T0043439

EDITOR'S LETTER

Mind matters

We've come a long way in relation to talking about neurodiversity, but there is still a long way to go says **JEMIMAH STEINFELD**

CENSORSHIP TAKES MANY forms, from jailed protesters and murdered journalists, to more subtle mechanisms, like societal pressures and norms that give some people more of a voice than others. It's with the latter in mind that we turn our attention to neurodiversity. The term was coined in the late 1990s to identify and promote the positives of variation in human thinking. Over the last few years it has become more widely used.

Given this, the Index team wanted to know whether neurodivergent people felt that the new term and the movement around it was helping them to have more of a voice and more agency? We wanted to know if old stereotypes were still rife? We wanted to know if information on and the perception of neurodiversity had improved? And if not was that because of censorship, overt or subtle? Finally, we wanted to know about all of this in a global context. Our team set to work.

Our first priority was to put neurodivergent voices front and centre,

so the majority of articles here are written by neurodivergent people. From these articles a fascinating picture emerges. Many said they did have more of a voice and that awareness had shot up. They greeted the word "neurodiversity" as empowering and welcomed a growth in onscreen representation.

At the same time it was clear that conversations around neurodiversity were playing out along society's current fault-lines and were far from immune. Social media has significantly improved connection for those who might otherwise feel sidelined, but as Morgan Barbour says it has given rise to a faker movement, to endless disinformation and to a lot of animosity. The latter was echoed by Nick Ransom, who highlighted social media pile-ons directed at "Autism Moms". Ransom added that autism continues to be used as a slur, only now often by those on the right to silence those on the "woke" left. And the actor Lillian Carrier told us of the fierce debate about who should represent a

neurodivergent person on-screen. Sadly in this debate sometimes the decision is no one.

Assumptions are also still being made about who is neurodivergent and who isn't - women's voices continue to be dismissed write Ashley Gjøvik and Meltem Ariken - and certain views of medical best practise dominate, silencing those who wish to challenge the orthodoxy and propose alternatives.

As somewhat expected, the picture in places like Brazil and Turkey was more bleak. The most alarming article came from Ugonna-Ora Owoh in Nigeria. He interviewed dyslexic people who had been taken to their local church to be exorcised, a trauma most had not shaken off.

Such a large topic ultimately needs more space than we have been able to give it. Still, we hope it challenges thinking about who and why certain people have a voice and what we collectively can do. More importantly we hope it's a launchpad for further enquiry and talk on neurodiversity. If we had one single takeaway from our research it would be that while conversations are happening more today than yesterday plenty more are needed still. ✖

Jemimah Steinfeld is Index editor-in-chief

52(02):1/1|DOI:10.1177/03064220231183793

'My mental health was at a very low point'

Introducing our cover artist

Charlotte Crawford, from Berkshire in the UK, rediscovered her love for art during Covid. "I had no job and my mental health was at a very low point," she said. After ending up in hospital, she was diagnosed as autistic aged 21. She says, "There is a lack of knowledge and understanding when it comes to autism. More and more people are aware of the struggles autistic people face on a day-to-day basis but there is still a long way to go." "'Powerful' is a mixed media artwork. I created this using minimal lines and bold blocks of colour. The repetitive lines were intended to mimic a fingerprint. I see links between the lines in the art and the natural lines in the centre of tree trunks."

CONTENTS

Up Front

1 MIND MATTERS:
   JEMIMAH STEINFELD
   The term neurodiversity has
   positively challenged how we
   approach our minds. Has it
   done enough?

6 THE INDEX: MARK FRARY
   The latest in free expression
   news, from an explainer on
   Sudan to a cha-cha-cha starring
   Meghan and King Charles

Features

14 BARS CAN'T STOP A
    BESTSELLER: KAYA GENÇ
    Fiction is finding its way
    out of a Turkish prison,
    says former presidential
    hopeful and bestselling writer
    Selahattin Demirtaş

17 DON'T MENTION
    FEMICIDE: CHRIS
    HAVLER-BARRETT
    Murdered women are
    an inconvenience for
    Mexico's president

20 THIS IS NO JOKE:
    QIAN GONG, JIAN XU
    The treatment of China's
    comedians is no laughing matter

24 SILENT DISCO:
    ANDREW MAMBONDIYANI
    Politicians are purging playlists
    in Zimbabwe, and musicians are
    speaking out

26 WHEN THE RUSSIANS
    CAME: ALINA SMUTKO,
    TARAS IBRAGIMOV,
    ALIONA SAVCHUK
    The view from inside occupied
    Crimea, through the cameras
    of photographers banned by
    the Kremlin

30 THE LANGUAGE OF
    WAR AND PEACE:

    JP O'MALLEY
    Kremlin-declared "Russophobe
    foreign agent and traitor"
    Mikhail Shishkin lays out the
    impossible choices for Russians

32 WRITER'S BLOCK:
    STACEY TSUI
    Hong Kong's journalists are
    making themselves heard, thanks
    to blockchain technology

34 THE RUSSIANS
    RISKING IT ALL:
    KATIE DANCEY-DOWNS
    Forced to sing songs and labelled
    as extremists, anti-war Russians
    are finding creative ways to take
    a stand

37 THE 'TRUTH' IS IN THE TEA:
    JEMIMAH STEINFELD
    Spilling the tea on a London
    venue, which found itself in hot
    water due to a far-right speaker

43 WAITING FOR CHINA'S
    TAP ON THE SHOULDER:
    CHU YANG

    However far they travel, there's
    no safe haven for journalists and
    academics who criticise China

44 WHEN THE OLD FOX
    WALKS THE TIGHTROPE:
    DANSON KAHYANA
    An interview with Stella
    Nyanzi on Uganda's latest
    anti-LGBTQ+ law

46 WOULD THE MEDIA
    LIE TO YOU?: ALI LATIFI
    Fake news is flourishing in
    Afghanistan, in ways people
    might not expect

48 BRITAIN'S HOLOCAUST
    ISLAND: MARTIN BRIGHT
    Confronting Britain's painful
    secret, and why we must
    acknowledge what happened on
    Nazi-occupied Alderney

53 THE THORN IN
    VIETNAM'S CIVIL
    SOCIETY SIDE: THIÊN VIỆT
    Responding to mass suppression
    with well-organised disruption

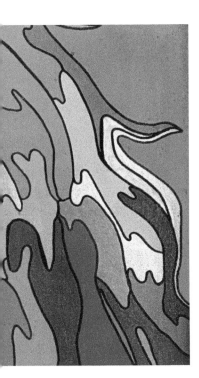

Special Report: Express yourself - Overcoming neurodiversity stereotypes

....

56 NOT A SLUR: **NICK RANSOM**
What's in a word? Exploring representation, and the power of the term "neurodiversity" to divide or unite

60 SIT DOWN, SHUT UP: **KATHARINE P BEALS**
The speech of autistic non-speakers is being hijacked

62 FAKE IT TILL YOU BREAK IT: **MORGAN BARBOUR**
Social media influencers are putting dissociative identity disorder in the spotlight, but some are accused of faking it

64 WEAPONISING DIFFERENCE: **SIMONE DIAS MARQUES**
Ableist slurs in Brazil are equating neurodivergence with criminality

66 AUTISM ON SCREEN IS GONNA BE OKAY: **KATIE DANCEY-DOWNS**
The Rain Man days are over. Everything's Gonna Be Okay star Lillian Carrier digs into autism on screen

68 RAISING MALAYSIA'S ROOF: **FRANCIS CLARKE**
In a comedy club in Malaysia's capital stand up is where people open up, says comedian Juliana Heng

70 LIVING IN THE SHADOWS: **ASHLEY GIØVIK**
When successful camouflage has a lasting impact

72 NIGERIA'S CRUCIBLE: **UGONNA-ORA OWOH**
Between silence and lack of understanding, Nigeria's neurodiverse are being mistreated

74 MY AUTISM IS NOT A LIE: **MELTEM ARIKAN**
An autism diagnosis at 52 liberated a dissident playwright, but there's no space for her truth in Turkey

Comment

....

78 LIVED EXPERIENCE, TO A POINT: **JULIAN BAGGINI**
When it comes to cultural debates, whose expertise carries the most weight?

80 FRANCE: ON THE ROAD TO ILLIBERALISM?: **JEAN-PAUL MARTHOZ**
Waving au revoir to the right to criticise

82 MONITORING TERRORISTS, GANGS – AND HISTORIANS: **ANDREW LOWNIE**
The researcher topping the watchlist on his majesty's secret service

84 WE ARE ALL DISSIDENTS: **RUTH ANDERSON**
Calls to disassociate from certain dissidents due to their country of birth are toxic and must be challenged

Culture

....

88 MANUSCRIPTS DON'T BURN: **REBECCA RUTH GOULD**
Honouring the writers silenced by execution in Georgia, and unmuzzling their voices

93 OBSCENELY FAMILIAR: **MARC NASH**
A book arguing for legalised homosexuality is the spark for a fiction rooted in true events

94 A TRULY GRAPHIC TALE: **ZOFEEN T EBRAHIM, TAHA SIDDIQUI**
A new graphic novel lays bare life on Pakistan's kill list, finding atheism and a blasphemous tattoo

98 A CENSORED DAY: **KAYA GENC**
Unravelling the questions that plague the censor, in a new short story from the Turkish author

102 POETRY'S PEACEBUILDING TENTACLES: **NATASHA TRIPNEY**
Literature has proven its powers of peace over the last decade in Kosovo

104 PALESTINE: I STILL HAVE HOPE: **BASSEM EID**
Turning to Israel and Palestine, where an activist believes the international community is complicit in the conflict

CREDIT: Charlotte Crawford

INDEXONCENSORSHIP.ORG

CHIEF EXECUTIVE
Ruth Anderson

EDITOR-IN-CHIEF
Jemimah Steinfeld

ASSISTANT EDITOR
Katie Dancey-Downs

EDITOR-AT-LARGE
Martin Bright

ASSOCIATE EDITOR
Mark Frary

ART DIRECTOR
Matthew Hasteley

EDITORIAL ASSISTANT
Francis Clarke

SUB EDITORS
Adam Aiken,
Tracey Bagshaw,
Jan Fox

HEAD OF POLICY & CAMPAIGNS
Jessica Ní Mhainín

POLICY & CAMPAIGNS OFFICER
Nik Williams

EVENTS &
PARTNERSHIPS MANAGER
Emma Sandvik Ling

DIRECTORS & TRUSTEES
Trevor Phillips (Chair),
Kate Maltby (Vice Chair),
Anthony Barling, Andrew Franklin,
James Goode, Elaine Potter,
Mark Stephens

PATRONS
Margaret Atwood, Simon Callow,
Steve Coogan, Brian Eno,
Christopher Hird, Jude Kelly,
Michael Palin, Matthew Parris,
Alexandra Pringle, Gabrielle Rifkind,
Sir Tom Stoppard, Lady Sue
Woodford Hollick

ADVISORY COMMITTEE
Julian Baggini, Clemency Bwurton-Hill,
Ariel Dorfman, Michael Foley,
Conor Gearty, AC Grayling,
Lyndsay Griffiths, William Horsley,
Anthony Hudson, Natalia Koliada,
Jane Kramer, Jean-Paul Marthoz,
Robert McCrum, Rebecca MacKinnon,
Beatrice Mtetwa, Julian Petley,
Michael Scammell, Kamila Shamsie,
Michael Smyth, Tess Woodcraft,
Christie Watson, Donaldson Trust

The Index

52(02):4/12|DOI:10.1177/03064220231183794

A round-up of events in the world of free expression from Index's unparalleled network of writers and activists

Edited by
MARK FRARY

PICTURED: Afghan men who sold their kidneys in an attempt to save their families from starvation show their operation scar marks in Sayshanba Bazar village in Herat province. Some of the Afghan journalists we are in touch with have considered doing the same

CREDIT: Wakil Kohsar/AFP

The Index

ELECTION WATCH

FRANCIS CLARKE looks at what is happening at the poll booths of the world

1. Poland

OCTOBER/NOVEMBER 2023

Polish citizens head to the polls in October or November, with the right-wing populist Law and Justice party (PiS) in power since 2015 and controlling both the presidency and the lower house of parliament. Part of a coalition of parties called the United Right, PiS is popular yet controversial, with media freedom under attack and a repeal of LGBTQ+ and abortion rights over the past few years. Donald Tusk, former Polish prime minister and former president of the European Council, hopes to head a liberal coalition to dislodge PiS. As a result, in what's been described as "straight out of the Trumpian playbook", President Andrzej Duda, without evidence, has warned of mass voter fraud during the election, and vowed a PiS member will be present at every polling station in the country as an observer.

2. Liberia

OCTOBER 2023

Liberian President George Weah will run for a second term in office in October 2023, but events of the past year threaten a show of support for the former footballer. Weah faced a backlash in 2022 as his government was mired in corruption allegations. The allegations, by the US Treasury, involved misuse of public funds by Weah's chief of staff, among others. Despite promising to fight corruption before he became president, the organisation Transparency International said Liberia is joint 142 out of 180 countries in its Corruption Perceptions Index. The Robert Lansing Institute for Global Threats and Democratic Studies believe Liberia has failed to reach critical benchmarks to ensure the elections are credible, and said the National Elections Commission, the body constitutionally mandated to supervise free and fair elections, "appears to be conducting its affairs as an extension of the ruling party and the government of President Weah". It cites delays in registration of voters, Liberia's voting systems being prone to fraud, and the refusal to transmit election results electronically to reduce human interference, as reasons for this.

3. Maldives

SEPTEMBER 2023

The Maldives government has proposed election law amendments that would prevent both foreign and freelance journalists from covering the country's national elections in September, fuelling suspicions about vote rigging. Only "registered journalists" – as described under the proposed changes to Section 41(a) and 41(b) of the country's General Elections Act – would be able to report, which means only journalists that work for government-approved media outlets. The Maldives Journalists Association expressed concerns it will reduce trust in the electoral process as it will curtail the media's opportunity to freely monitor the election. The Maldives has had a past troubled relationship with journalists. In 2018, the previous government tried to prevent news coverage of opposition demonstrations and activities. Last year, under President Ibrahim Mohamed Solih, the government introduced a provision in law which forces journalists to give up their sources if requested. Journalists who refuse to disclose a source can be found in contempt, and face up to three months in jail or be fined. ✖

LEFT TO RIGHT: (Poland) President Andrzej Duda; (Liberia) President George Weah; (Maldives) President Ibrahim Mohamed Solih

Ink spot

JOURNALIST SHAMSUZZAMAN SHAMS of the leading Bangladeshi daily newspaper Prothom Alo was detained this spring by the country's authorities after he wrote an article on the rising cost of living. The authorities argued that the piece "smeared the government" and he now faces charges under Bangladesh's draconian Digital Security Act. If convicted, he could spend seven years in prison. He's currrently on bail.

Ahmed Kabir Kishore, the Bangladeshi cartoonist who drew this, has also been a target of the Act for his work. While he was held in custody in May 2020, Kishore says he was severely tortured alongside the writer Mushtaq Ahmed. Ahmed died in jail in 2021 and Kishore was released shortly afterwards.

In our Index Index mapping the free expression landscape across the globe, Bangladesh is ranked in the second lowest category for both media and digital freedoms.

Free speech in numbers

52,000

The number of people in the crowd at a match between Arsenal and Newcastle United, now owned by Saudi-state owned PIF, who witnessed a plane flying over St James' Park, London, carrying a banner calling for the release of all Saudi prisoners of conscience, organised by human rights organisation Sanad

72 The age of Syrian human rights defender Jdea Abdullah Nawfal, executive director of the Syrian Center for Democracy and Civil Rights, who was viciously attacked in the city of Al-Suwayda by an unidentified assailant in early May, suffering multiple fractures and a deep wound to the head

51 The number of weeks protesters can spend in jail if they lock on to another person, object or land causing serious disruption to two or more people under the UK's new Public Order Act 2023, introduced just days before King Charles III's coronation

5 Length of sentence in years, including hard labour, handed to Kuwaiti blogger Salman Al-Khalidi in absentia for "intentionally [spreading] false and malicious rumours abroad about the country's internal conditions, publishing what would harm relations of Kuwait with other countries". In January, he had an earlier five-year sentence for similar charges pardoned by the Emir of Kuwait

1,477

The number of book bans in the USA in the first half of the 2022-23 academic year, according to PEN America

The Index

PEOPLE WATCH

FRANCIS CLARKE highlights the stories of human rights defenders under attack

Iryna Horobtsova

UKRAINE

Iryna Horobtsova is a human rights defender from Kherson. Horobtsova volunteered to transport supplies and workers to the local hospital during the Russian occupation of the city. After posting on social media about peaceful rallies against the occupation, she was abducted from her home by the Russian military at the end of May 2022. After Ukraine regained Kherson, Horobtsova's parents were told she'd been transferred to Russian-occupied Crimea. Horobtsova's last reported sighting was in prison in Crimea.

Yang Maodong

CHINA

Known by his pen name Guo Feixiong, Yang Maodong is a lawyer and human rights activist. In May, a court in Guangzhou sentenced Yang to eight years imprisonment for "inciting subversion of state power". Yang said he would appeal. He was arrested in December 2021 after earlier being denied access to visit his ill wife in the USA. According to the Guardian, Yang said the sentence was "score settling" for his long-term rights advocacy, and the court accused him of publishing "seditious" material online.

Muhammed Yavaş

TURKEY

In the run up to the first round of Turkey's May 2023 general elections, journalist Muhammed Yavaş was attacked and assaulted in the town of Çan by Hasan Dinç, the head of the local branch of the pro-government Grey Wolves nationalist group. After publishing a post online criticising political banners by the group, Yavaş was invited to meet Dinç at a local café, who subsequently attacked him. Dinç has claimed he was provoked, an allegation that Yavaş denies. Yavaş has since filed a criminal complaint against Dinç.

Anousa "Jack" Luangsouphom

LAOS

Luangsouphom is a social media activist, who was shot twice at a bar in the country's capital Vientiane on 29 April 2023. Initially reported as a fatal attack, Luangsouphom survived the ordeal, which was carried out by an unknown assailant. Luangsouphom runs two Facebook pages devoted to advocating for rights in Laos. One of the pages calls for an end to the one-party rule, where attacks and reprisals faced by political human rights defenders are commonplace.

Index launches new UK Anti-SLAPP Coalition website

THE UK ANTI-SLAPP Coalition's new website has been launched and can be found at **antislapp.uk**, which was led by Index on Censorship and supported by Open Society Foundations. The website showcases how the coalition has grown from an idea to an engaged network of over 20 organisations who have helped shape the agenda and have spoken to MPs, parliamentary committees and representatives from the Ministry of Justice about the need to stamp out SLAPPs (strategic lawsuits against public participation). The problem with SLAPPs is that too much happens beyond public view - the threatening letter or email exchanges, the drawn-out pre-trial negotiations, the lengthy court proceedings (if it ever gets that far). The website seeks to shine a light on the tactics used and showcase a number of SLAPPs cases, such as those directed at Carole Cadwalladr, Tom Burgis, Realtid and many more.

Nik Williams, policy and campaigns officer at Index, said:

"The site is a vital resource that will serve as a repository for everything related to SLAPPs. SLAPP claimants win when targets are isolated, but the coalition exists to tell them that they are not alone. There is a group of experts from across civil society ready to support and stand in solidarity with them."

The website also highlights the ways out of this mess, from sharing the Model Anti-SLAPP law that the coalition drafted with support from legal and industry experts to highlighting how targets of SLAPPs can complain to the Solicitors Regulation Authority (SRA) and how the Council of Europe can be informed of SLAPP actions aimed at journalists.

World In Focus: Sudan

Conflict persists in Sudan as the country's two biggest armed groups, the Sudanese Armed Forces and the paramilitary Rapid Support Forces, wrestle for power. Free expression is also coming under attack in this conflict

1 Nyala

Journalists came under fire as police attacked a camp for displaced people affected by the conflict. Police reportedly fired tear gas and assaulted people at the El-Geer camp near the city of Nyala in southwest Sudan, ignoring aid agencies who were present. There were also numerous reports that journalists had been trapped nationwide during fighting, often with shortages of food and water. This includes 15 journalists trapped inside the Sudan News Agency building on 14 April 2023 for three days, after clashes in the capital, Khartoum, according to the International Federation of Journalists. These events not only affected the safety of journalists, but also the ability to carry out their work to provide civilians with information.

2 Khartoum

Both Abdel Fattah Al-Burhan, leader of the SAF, and Mohamed Hamdan Dagalo, commander of the RSF, have been accused of spreading disinformation through the media during the conflict. Fighting raged near the state television headquarters in Khartoum, which forced transmission to be cut, meaning Twitter and Facebook becoming key sources of information and false information was easily spread. After Twitter removed legacy blue ticks, a fake account with a verified blue tick claiming to represent the RSF falsely claimed Hamdan Dagalo had died, with Twitter's own public metrics claiming it had been viewed around a million times (the real RSF Twitter account doesn't have a verified blue tick). Additionally, researchers at the Atlantic Council – working with data from Beam Reports, which investigates disinformation in Sudan – identified around 900 Twitter

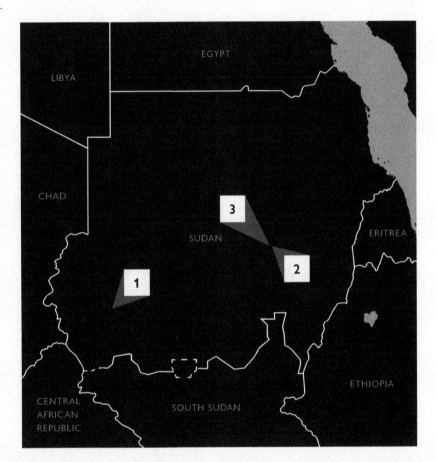

accounts that looked to be artificially sharing RSF messages on social media. Also, some circulating images and photos on social media that claimed to be fighting in Sudan were found to include footage of conflicts in Yemen or Libya.

3 Ombdurman

While the conflict has resulted in risks to freedom of expression, it has worsened Sudan's already poor record in the area. Immediately after the 2021 military coup, when Fattah Al-Burhan gained power, at least three people died, and several were injured when security forces opened fire

on pro-democracy protests in the city of Ombdurman. Political killings and the targeting of civil society organisations have also increased. According to Article 19's 2022 Global Expression Report, Sudan was placed in the lowest category possible, being recorded as "in crisis". In Reporters without Borders 2023 World Press Freedom Index, the country was placed 148 out of 180 countries. Sudan's Cybercrime Law, introduced in 2018, has been used to limit access to online news websites, and an amendment in 2022 aimed to imprison offenders where the victim of defamation or fake news was a governmental public figure.

The Index

TECH WATCH

GOD SAVE THE KING... AND THE REST OF US – FROM AI

Some say you can tell a fake photo from the teeth, but we're not so confident. **MARK FRARY** reports on the perils of AI-generated images

THE MOST ARRESTING pictures emerging from the coronation of King Charles III in early May were, perhaps surprisingly, not those of members of the anti-monarchy organisation Republic being detained by police. But a quick word on that: Republic CEO Graham Smith and five others were held for supposedly carrying devices that would enable them to "lock-on" and disrupt the procession, which the Met Police now "regrets". It was a dark day for the UK's free speech record.

The images of yellow Abolish the Monarchy placards and T-shirts against the gilt (or should that be guilt) of the royal carriage were striking but not the images that went viral.

The images in question were instead the very personal shots of the King, Queen Camilla, William and Kate, as well as Harry and Meghan at celebrations following the event. Wait, what? Did you say Meghan? I thought she wasn't there, you say.

RIGHT: A scene that never happened, created by AI of Charles III dancing with Meghan at a coronation afterparty

Yes, quite. You see the pictures from the coronation "afterparty" are not actually real – they were created using artificial intelligence by an Australian design agency.

Perth-based Start Design used the AI tool Midjourney "to create a set of (kinda) real photos from an imagined party at Windsor Palace. By using prompts detailing the camera angle, frame, ISO, aperture, lighting style and camera type, we were able to get a set of images that felt pretty close to the real thing. Who knew the King got moves…"

The images were viewed millions of times on TikTok and Facebook and received blanket traditional media coverage.

The design agency's intentions were to demonstrate the power of AI tools like Midjourney rather than to deceive, but the quality of the images show just how easy that can be.

Indeed, in the same week that the afterparty images emerged, Amnesty International was forced to apologise for using images to promote a new report on police brutality in Colombia during 2021 protests. One of the images showed a young woman being dragged away by police. But the image was not what it seemed. A close look revealed that both police and protester have oddly warped faces, while the uniforms and insignia on them were incorrect.

These images too had been produced by AI. After an outcry, Amnesty removed the images from social media.

Erika Guevara Rosas, director for the Americas at Amnesty, told The Guardian, "We don't want the criticism

for the use of AI-generated images to distract from the core message in support of the victims and their calls for justice in Colombia…But we do take the criticism seriously and want to continue the engagement to ensure we understand better the implications and our role to address the ethical dilemmas posed by the use of such technology."

Like everything AI, these images throw up questions and concerns. The coronation afterparty images generated by AI, for example, are strikingly similar to the incredible photographs meticulously created by the artist Alison Jackson, a judge in our Freedom of Expression Awards last year. Rather than using AI, Jackson uses the world's best lookalikes to create imagined scenes, including many with the Royal Family. While some people have been upset with her portrayals – and have tried to squash them – we support them as both art and social satire at its finest. So why not the same with AI?

The crux of the matter is what the viewer believes – and also what the intention is. As AI tools improve, the difficulty in separating fact from fiction will become more and more challenging, and this is something bad actors could very easily take advantage of.

In May, the Irish Times was forced to apologise after it ran an opinion piece by a Dublin-based Ecuadorian health worker, which berated Irish women who used fake tan for mocking people of colour. The article turned out to have been written by AI writing tool ChatGPT with AI-generated images to back it up. The person behind the article

was lying, very deliberately, and the Irish Times fell for it.

A month earlier, Kuwait News shared a video of their new female presenter "Fedha". Speaking in Arabic, she said: "I'm Fedha, the first presenter in Kuwait who works with artificial intelligence at Kuwait News. What kind of news do you prefer? Let's hear your opinions." Fedha is not real but generated by AI. The presenter's name means "silver", a subtle reference to the metallic skin of robots. Kuwait News said the presenter was AI-generated but it is easy to see from the coronation images that these things travel fast and often without the explanatory information. Would-be conspiracy theorists are undoubtedly using these tools already.

Such AI confections pose an ethical dilemma. What is real? Can those caught in compromising positions now claim that the images were generated by AI and they have nothing to hide? Can dictators dismiss Amnesty and other NGOs more easily with the label "fake news"? And what can we do?

Some have suggested one answer lies in watermarking or tagging the image or video metadata to indicate that the image was not captured in real life. Sadly that too can be faked. Perhaps technology provides an answer. Blockchain, which underlies cryptocurrencies such as Bitcoin, offers a way of creating an unalterable digital ledger of transactions, which could include details related to the creation of photos. Because it is decentralised it will give us all a role in keeping track of what is a true record of an event.

Ultimately, if the truth is to survive, our only choice might be to regulate for tighter controls, and get more tech savvy in the process. ✖

Mark Frary is associate editor at Index

A close look revealed that both police and protester have oddly warped faces

The Index

MY INSPIRATION

A WINK OF HOPE

ARIEL DORFMAN remembers a small but meaningful gesture from one of the many inspiring figures who risked it all during the 1973 coup in Chile

HOW EASY TO name those who shine, immediately recognisable as soon as one speaks their syllables – Mandela, Lincoln, Mozart and two Rosas, Parks and Luxembourg – but I'd rather focus on those nobody knows or remembers, the supposedly negligible humans who make history anonymously, day by day, minute by minute. And it is less than a minute, in fact, that I return to over and over, for inspiration.

It is a few days after the coup in Chile that, on 11 September 1973, overthrew Salvador Allende – and how he does inspire me as he makes his last stand at the Presidential Palace in defence of democracy and justice – and I am trying to survive, I am being hunted by the military, I am heading on foot towards a plaza in Santiago to meet my inspirational wife Angélica so she can indicate a safe house where to hide. I cannot shake my depression– everything I dreamt of is being destroyed, friends are being tortured and murdered, my country's hopes dashed, and it is then, at what must be one of the saddest moments of my life, that I cross a man walking in the opposite direction. He's an Allendista, from the working class, we recognise each other immediately as compañeros. Though we've never met, I've seen thousands like him in marches and rallies, factories and shantytowns. He seems to understand by my tormented face what I am going through, and as we pass each other, he winks. No more than that: an eye that shuts and opens, shuts like our peaceful revolution that is being crushed and then opens, like a message from the future he is sending. Telling me: you are not alone, we shall overcome these bitter days, people like me, we have been repressed since birth, yet here I am, we will make history together. Fifty years later, that wink still inspires me. ✖

Ariel Dorfman is a Chilean-American author and human rights activist, whose books have been published in over 50 languages and plays performed in over 100 countries. Among his works are Death and the Maiden and forthcoming novel, The Suicide Museum

PICTURED: Salvador Allende waves to his supporters on 11 September 1973, around 40 minutes before rebels, led by Pinochet, started shooting at the Presidential Palace in Santiago

CREDIT: Pierre Crom/Getty

FEATURES

"Just eight Jews are officially recorded as dying on Alderney. Secunda, who describes himself as a researcher as well as an artist, is sceptical"

MARTIN BRIGHT | BRITAIN'S HOLOCAUST ISLAND | P.48

Bars can't stop a bestseller

Speaking from prison, author and politician **SELAHATTIN DEMIRTAŞ** tells **KAYA GENÇ** that Turkey's jails can't stop him resisting

"IT'S MY SIXTH year in prison, and this is my fifth book written from prison," notes the Kurdish politician and author Selahattin Demirtaş in the acknowledgments section of DAD, the latest volume of short stories he has written behind bars.

"I didn't aim to become an author and publish numerous books when I set out to write. But, in time, this turned into an issue of stubbornness. The longer they keep me inside this 12-square-metre cell, the more I'll pursue my adventures in literature."

In an exclusive interview with Index, Demirtaş emphasised his determination to continue working from behind bars.

"I've spent years working as a human rights defender and lawyer, focusing on civil rights," he said from his cell in Edirne Prison. "Freedom of expression is the mother of all rights. Without it, you can't defend or improve any other right. Even the right to life can't be adequately defended and protected without the freedom of expression."

When Demirtaş was detained in a dawn raid at his house in Diyarbakır in November 2016 – along with more than 10 MPs from the leftist political movement he led – nobody predicted he would spend the next six years behind

> ## Without free thought, a society can't exist or defend itself

bars. Known as the Kurdish Obama by his admirers, he was accused of instigating riots to protest Isis attacks against the Kurds in the northern Syrian town of Kobane in 2014.

As the co-leader of the progressive Peoples' Democratic Party (HDP), Demirtaş was a star: a funny, warm, handsome politician in his early 40s with a penchant for ruffling feathers among the political classes.

He ran a colourful presidential campaign in 2014, when he came third with 9.77% of the vote. In the June 2015 general election, Demirtaş's popularity helped the HDP come in fourth place with 13.12% of the vote. This was the first time the pro-Kurdish party had presented itself as a party for the whole of Turkey, a strategy that allowed it to enter parliament by passing the 10% electoral threshold thanks to votes coming from dissidents not only among Kurds but among all ethnicities.

The fact that Turkey's president, Recep Tayyip Erdoğan, chose to prosecute Demirtaş a year later wasn't surprising. (The Constitutional Court was finalising its decision on whether to shut down the party this April.)

In March 2015, Demirtaş gave a historic speech of just three sentences: "We'll not make you president. We'll not make you president. We'll not make you president." He was targeting Erdoğan's plans of becoming an executive president and turning Turkey into a Latin American-style *presidencialismo*. There was jubilation and cheers in the HDP's parliamentary group session where Demirtaş gave the speech.

ABOVE: Selahattin Demirtaş giving a speech at a rally organised by his party in Siirt, Turkey in 2014

Demirtaş hasn't written a memoir of his rise to political stardom and imprisonment yet, but in 2017 he surprised supporters by publishing Dawn, a book of short stories. He explained that it was his wife, Başak, who convinced him to write fiction. She visited him each week, travelling from their family home in Diyarbakır to Edirne (a 1,686km journey from the east of Turkey to the western border) and encouraging him to polish his stories for publication. His debut, which sold 200,000 copies in four months, is

CREDIT: Halkların Demokratik Partisi - HDP

dedicated to "all women who have been murdered or victims of violence". The 12 stories depict men subjecting women to various forms of violence: physical, psychological and emotional.

"I don't start writing my stories to highlight the women's struggle particularly," Demirtaş said. "Yet when I work on their plots, structures and characters, the issue of gender and equality arises, and I don't refrain from projecting my point of view in those moments. I consider the women's struggle an inherent part of the struggle for labour rights, environment, freedom and peace." These concerns, he added, have been shaping "all my life, practice, actions and discourse".

Demirtaş explained how he spent years in the human rights struggle as a pro-bono lawyer before devoting 12 years to parliamentary politics. "In all those experiences, I had the opportunity to meet thousands of victims face-to-face. I learned about their stories and contributed to their struggles for rights. I observed how women encountered gender-based oppression. I watched their determined struggles and tried supporting them in my way."

He said this experience taught him that problems about political power "can't be solved without achieving gender equality", adding: "This is why the women's struggle plays a big role in the stories and novels I've written."

In the titular story of Demirtaş's new collection, DAD, a group of women conspire to kill men who intimidate and rape women. These are charismatic figures well-versed in foreign languages and martial arts (an illustration of a woman wearing a motorcycle helmet, black gloves and a purple feminist scarf adorns the book's cover), and they use social media and dating apps to trap their prey. The story reads like a detective tale, inspiring readers to figure out the identity of the angel of vengeance.

In Kurdish, "dad" means "revenge"; it is also the initials of the women working in solidarity to right wrongs.

Demirtaş is an intriguing cultural figure in Turkey. After his first novel, Leylan – a sci-fi love story about a brain surgeon's tragic attempt to enter her husband's mind – was published in 2019, a lawyer working for the State Railways of Turkey was taken to a police station. A colleague informed on him for keeping a copy of the book in his office drawer. Even the PTT, Turkey's postal service, refused to carry the book.

Still, the interest proved impossible to ignore. Dawn sold more than 220,000 copies, and readers waited six hours at a book fair where 20 famous authors signed Demirtaş's books in solidarity. DAD became the top-selling book as soon as it was released on 10 March: in 20 days, eight editions were published and 100,000 copies were sold. In the branches of two big bookstore chains, Remzi and Penguen, the book received the JK Rowling treatment, with mountains of copies stacked at the entrance. (D&R, owned by a group with ties to the government, refused to sell the book in at least one of its branches.)

Yet DAD's popularity raised the alarm among the government ranks. Eleven days after its publication, the Radio and Television Council fined Halk TV, one of the few networks not owned by Erdoğan supporters, for running a positive review of DAD on air. Accused of praising a criminal, Halk TV had to pay millions from its advertisement →

LEFT: Selahattin Demirtaş pictured back in 2014, before he was unjustly incarcerated

→ revenue to the council and was banned from running further programmes.

Despite losing his freedom at home, Demirtaş's reach expanded outside Turkey. In December 2018, the actor Sarah Jessica Parker, of Sex and the City fame, was spotted carrying a copy of Dawn in Brooklyn. The Mail Online reported that the "actress added large black sunglasses while holding the book Dawn: Stories. She seems to have obtained an advance copy as the book does not come out until April 2019". (The book's English edition came from Parker's imprint, SJP for Hogarth.)

Maureen Freely, the novelist, translator and a former head of English PEN, wrote the book's introduction and noted how Dawn was part of a "grand tradition" of prison literature in Turkey, listing the poet Nâzım Hikmet and the novelists Orhan Kemal, Sevgi Soysal and Yaşar Kemal as his literary predecessors.

Those voices devoted their lives "to those who could imagine a world beyond the injustices of authoritarian rule", Freely wrote.

"If there is a topic called 'prison literature' in a country, then that country has a deep-rooted system of oppression," Demirtaş said. "Unfortunately, prison literature has grown into a vast corpus in Turkey. Since the republic's foundation in 1923, there has not been one year where

Thoughts are but fantasies if they aren't articulated in words or actions

intellectuals, authors, journalists or artists haven't spent time in prisons. Intellectuals are dissident by nature, and in Turkey the most dangerous thing is to be opposed to the system."

He noted how "thousands have turned into authors in prison" there. "When I entered the prison, I was a politician and a lawyer. In six-and-a-half years, I wrote five books, so I guess I can also be considered a prison author now. While prisons are designed as spaces of punishment and destruction, we're struggling to transform these spaces into centres of production and resistance."

He characterised his new vocation as a "different method of resistance against oppression", one that made sure "we can protect ourselves inside the prison system through meaningful acts", and allowed them "to keep our will strong".

Demirtaş compared the current era in Turkey to the Middle Ages. "Just because of my speeches and social media posts, I've been held in this cell for the past six-and-a-half years, and I answer your questions from here. The situation is so ironic."

He stressed the importance of freedom of expression. "Thoughts are but fantasies if they aren't articulated in words or actions. But if they encounter prosecution when articulated or acted upon, thoughts lose their meaning." He said there "won't be, can't be, any progression or development" in a country that suppresses free expression, and asked international bodies and organisations to be "always on alert" about the cases in Turkey.

"Without free thought, a society can't exist or defend itself." ✖

Kaya Genç is Index's Turkey contributor. He is based in Istanbul

52(02):14/16|DOI:10.1177/03064220231183795

Don't mention femicide

The Mexican government no longer wants to hear about the femicide crisis facing the country because it is politically inconvenient. But obscuring the truth doesn't make it go away, writes **CHRIS HAVLER-BARRETT**

ABOVE: Friends of Debanhi Escobar, an 18-year-old law student who went missing on April 2022 and was found dead inside a water tank, amid a spate of disappearances of women in Mexico, pay homage to her, 25 April 2022

CREDIT: Daniel Becerril/Reuters/Alamy

EVERY MARCH MEXICO turns purple. City guides attribute this phenomenon to the jacaranda tree, which coats the capital in blossom reminiscent of Japan in the springtime. But it is not only the jacaranda that is responsible for this flood of purple. Across doors, walls, statues, gates, fences and municipal buildings, the slogan *Ni una menos* (Not one less) is daubed in vibrant purple paint, surrounded by posters of the missing and the dead. Faces of women – almost all of them young – stare out from the page, with names, details and accusations written large.

Mexico is a country that is no stranger to brutality. There have been 151,708 murders since President Andrés Manuel López Obrador – known as Amlo – took power in 2018. Much of the violence can be squarely blamed on the drugs war that is tearing the country apart – a civil war bubbling just out of sight. But a vein of aggressive chauvinism that runs through the country has led to thousands of women being killed simply for the crime of not being born male. Many of these killings are never investigated. Most are perpetrated simply out of anger against women.

The World Health Organisation defines femicide as "intentional murder of women because they are women". Here, this is a crime that happens every few hours.

The brutality against women, which is almost casual in its frequency, is as shocking as any cartel killing. In February 2020, 25-year-old Ingrid Escamilla was found skinned. In the same week, seven-year-old Fatima Aldrighetti was kidnapped, raped and murdered. Debanhi Escobar took a taxi home from a party in 2022 and was found almost two weeks later, her corpse hidden inside a water tank.

The Secretariat for Protection and Security of Citizens states that 3,890 women were killed by homicide (which in Mexico includes cases of manslaughter) in 2022, of which 2,808

> ## Pretending the problem does not exist will not be enough to save their lives

were murders. Of these, only 1,075 were classified as femicides. Killings reached a peak during the pandemic, with 10 women a day losing their lives. Officially, 2022 saw an average of "only" three women a day killed in femicides – and the government says that numbers have decreased 35% since 2021.

As with so many statistics in Mexico, this is little more than propaganda. While the headline number is down, this is not necessarily reflective of the situation that women find themselves in. The femicide problem has reduced since Obrador took office, but not before first rising to record-breaking levels. More than 4,000 women have officially been killed in femicides since he assumed the presidency.

Government sources happily report the reduction in killings compared with the 2018 levels, but deliberately fail to mention the significant overall rise that has marred the majority of the Amlo administration. And this →

ABOVE: Women hold a protest ahead of the Day of the Dead against gender violence and femicide in Mexico City, October 2022

→ number is still inaccurate, as many such crimes are never reported or do not fit the legal definition of what can be considered a femicide.

Mexico introduced femicide laws to combat the rising wave of killings under former president Enrique Peña Nieto. These laws were designed to provide a framework for prosecutors to lay more serious charges but have, in effect, had an exclusionary effect on cases

of femicide that do not fit the model. Women who work on the front line of the femicide epidemic are exasperated by the barriers to justice that exist in a legal system that often does not care about what is happening.

The murder of a woman – whether by an intimate partner, a co-worker, a man in a position of authority or even a brutal attack by a stranger – is often not considered as a possible femicide by authorities. Many times, even killings that do fit the criteria are simply ignored.

Alexa Mendivil, a criminal lawyer from Mexico City, explains that

despite the fact the government treats femicide cases differently, the law itself is fundamentally unable to capture the extent of the violence being perpetrated.

"The problem in Mexico is not only impunity but apparent incompetence," she said. "On many occasions, I have experienced policemen and prosecutors failing to take immediate action and they do not keep the offended informed of their fundamental human rights.

"As a litigator, I have experienced at first-hand the lack of resources and the inability of the police to investigate a crime … most of the time leaving the

CREDIT: Raquel Cunha/Reuters/Alamy

burden of proof to the offended."

The government released updated guidelines in April, increasing penalties – especially against those who attack children – but many of the reforms will take time to implement, and there is little to compel police and prosecutors to act.

Cristina Flores works as a psychologist in a woman's prison, and often deals with the aftermath of violence. "It is much easier ... for the government to classify these [killings] as murders, because if they are catalogued as femicides it affects government statistics," she said.

"In cases where murders are reclassified as femicides, it is because the family of the victim, or the friends of the victim, or the neighbours of the victim, fight for a long time and raise their voices to say: 'This wasn't a murder, this was a femicide and you have everything you need to classify it as such'.

"It seems to me that it is a lot easier for the government to classify [a death] as a homicide because that way it does not put in danger the way that the rest of the world sees Mexico because of the levels of femicide." Flores says that women who fight off their attackers often find themselves jailed for assault, while the men walk free.

Ultimately, the problems in Mexico persist because the government aggressively rejects negative publicity. There is little action that the president is willing to take lest it detract from his legacy, other than to deflect and blame opposition politicians for lying about achievements, or promoting defective moral values that lead to these killings.

Those who question the official narrative are derided as enemies of Mexico. Amlo himself has accused those who protest femicide of being "conservatives" and of being agents employed by nefarious forces opposed to his government.

Mendivil feels that there has been a deliberate campaign to "to minimise the Mexican feminist movement [by] arguing it has become a conservative movement and opposition to his administration".

"[Amlo] lacks empathy for women's causes, which he does not comprehend and therefore fails to sympathise with. In a live conference, he even mistakenly equated femicide with homicide and attributed its causes to family disintegration on the International Day for the Elimination of Violence against Women," she said.

This dismissal of campaigners is effective. A recent survey of the president's popularity found that he was by far the most popular among those with no or sub-primary education.

The government aggressively rejects negative publicity

The survey also reported that 51% of Mexicans have full confidence in him and believe entirely in his mission. A further 17% of respondents said they generally had confidence in him.

This confidence means that he retains the ability to determine what 68% of Mexicans believe to be the truth. As he has downplayed the extent of the violence facing women, he is able to convince the majority of citizens that femicide is an issue that is used by an immoral minority determined to carry out a personal vendetta against him.

A recent leaked audio file directly links the president to efforts to close the National Institute for Transparency for the remainder of his term as president.

Obrador has also announced that he intends to abolish national news agency Notimex – which, while imperfect, provides a comparatively impartial news service. He has said the company is unnecessary as he now gives a personal news conference every weekday morning.

A recent survey by the National Institute for Statistics revealed that Mexicans felt significantly safer in 2023, despite the fact that violence is once again rising in the country. This sexenio – the six-year presidential term – has already been the most violent on record, and there are almost two years remaining.

Murder has risen in the first half of the year, but without free access to information the problem can be ignored. Unfortunately for thousands of women each year, pretending the problem does not exist will not be enough to save their lives. ✖

Chris Havler-Barrett is a freelance journalist based in Mexico

52(02):17/19|DOI:10.1177/03064220231183796

This is no joke

In China a comedian risks jail time for mocking the army. **QIAN GONG** and **JIAN XU** chart the rapid rise and potential fall of stand-up in the country

HUMOUR AND POLITICS are always a dangerous mix in authoritarian states and no more so than in China. A recent high-profile event that involved the punishment of popular stand-up comedian Li Haoshi and XiaoGuo Comedy, China's largest talk show company that hired Li and many of China's best-known stand-up comedians, proves that delivering a wrong punchline can have dire consequences: XiaoGuo has been fined colossal amounts of money (13.35 million yuan; $1.8 million) and Li possibly faces years in jail.

Performing under the English stage name House on 13 May this year, Li quipped that he adopted two stray dogs that turned out to be extremely energetic and capable. Once set free in the mountains, the dogs chased a squirrel like a missile launched into the air. Li then said he was so impressed that eight words came into his mind immediately: 作风优良, 能打胜仗, literally meaning they "can defeat enemies while maintaining excellent discipline and moral conduct", which is a typical slogan to praise China's People's Liberation Army in the Xi Jinping era. The punchline served its purpose and caused roaring laughter. However, some audiences felt very uncomfortable with Li's insult to the PLA. His joke was recorded by one of the audience members and posted on Sina Weibo, the most popular Chinese social media platform. The disclosed video soon sparked public outcry among netizens against Li and his company.

People accused Li of intentionally tarnishing the image of military soldiers and mocking Xi's political slogan. They believe Li's punchline alluded to a scene in the Red Classic propaganda film produced in 1956, Battle on Shangganling Mountain, in which People's Voluntary Army soldiers in the Korean War chased squirrels for fun in between battles. Moreover,

> People accused Li of intentionally tarnishing the image of military soldiers and mocking Xi's political slogan

ABOVE: Actors perform crosstalk at a temple fair in Beijing, 2017

the eight words he used to praise the stray dogs are the exact words Chinese president Xi said at the plenary meeting of the PLA delegation in 2013, which has now become a political slogan of the PLA.

As anger spiralled online, Xinhua News Agency and People's Daily, two of the biggest state media outlets,

issued online commentaries, criticising the comedian and reiterating that insulting the PLA is intolerable. The China Association of Performing Arts called for its members to boycott Li, according to the Management Measures for the Self-Disciplines of Arts in the Performing Arts Industry. Though Li and XiaoGuo both quickly apologised on social media, their apologies gained no forgiveness from either the public or the government. On top of the hefty fine, XiaoGuo was banned from future performances. Li's Weibo account was banned. The Chaoyang Branch of the Beijing Municipal Public Security filed a case to investigate the comedian due to what they perceived as the very harmful social impact that the incident caused. Li is likely to be accused of violating the Law on the Protection of the Status and Rights and Interests of Military Personnel of China, issued in 2021, and likely to face criminal prosecution.

Operating under strong censorship in China's cultural industries, performing arts that rely on humour have always walked a fine line between pleasing both audiences and regulatory bodies. While open political criticism on stage has never been possible, traditional two-people comic talk shows called "crosstalk", alongside more conventional comic skits, became popular amongst Chinese audiences on TV and on radio. During the 1980s to early 2000s they managed to carve out space to poke fun at social ills, even on the stage of the annual Spring Festival Gala live broadcast by the China Central Television, which has millions of viewers. For example, a crosstalk show called The Thief PTY Ltd satirised the prevalent social phenomenon of bureaucracy and nepotism, while star comedian Zhao Benshan's comic skit Uncle Niu's Promotion aired at the 1995 Spring Festival Gala and lampooned the social malaise of civil servants feasting on public funds. In this particular skit, a villager was "promoted" to director of a public service department due to

A crosstalk show called The Thief PTY Ltd satirised the prevalent social phenomenon of bureaucracy and nepotism

his ability to hold down alcohol. These critical comedy works became classics for millions of Chinese.

But the small space for fun has been squeezed in the last decade under Xi, as artists are expected to promote "positive energy" and morally educate the public. This has directly caused the decline in popularity of cross-talk and comic skits, as well as the CCTV Spring Festival Gala iself.

It was against this backdrop that stand-up comedy shows sprang up and gained popularity, especially in metropolitan cities such as Beijing and Shanghai and especially amongst millennials.

Watching stand-up comedy has become a popular middle-class leisure activity in China. In 2021 alone, China had 18,500 stand-up comedy shows and box office income had reached 391 million yuan ($55.4 million). This represents phenomenal growth for a burgeoning industry, considering live stand-up comedy only really started to emerge in China around 2014. In the years that have followed open mics and stand-up comedy competitions have gained huge traction offline and also on. Take the show Rock & Roast as an example. In Rock & Roast amateur comics compete against each other to become "talk king". An average of 70 million viewers watched the two-hour programme in 2019, up from 50 →

ABOVE: The comedian Li Haoshi performing his standup

→ million in 2017, and its Weibo page attracted up to six billion views by 2021.

Scholars Dan Chen and Gengsong Gao critically analysed the popularity of stand-up comedy and its politics in China in an article published in Critical Discourse Studies in 2021. They argue that stand-up comedies carefully transgressed and expanded the boundary of state rhetoric by providing alternative views on social issues of common concern in a subtle way. Their popularity for both performers and viewers was partly tied to their ability to be an arena in which people could speak more freely.

Sadly the incident of Li Haoshi shows the limitation of such "transgressive rhetoric", as well as the shrinking of the tiny areas of freedom for making jokes

An average of 70 million viewers watched the two-hour programme in 2019

in China today. With tightening control and regulation of artistic creation and of artists, more and more red lines have been drawn. Under Xi, Party-endorsed heroes, role models and official narratives of revolutionary events have become much more sensitive topics than they used to be. Ultimately they cannot be easily mocked or deconstructed. People who cross the line see their works or speeches labelled as "historical nihilism" and get punished.

The Li incident is not the first time comedians in China's rising stand-up scene have found themselves in hot water. In 2019 former Chinese men's football team captain Fan Zhiyi mocked the disappointing performance of the Chinese men's basketball team in the 2019 Basketball World Cup in an episode in Rock & Roast Season Five and was criticised by Xinhua News Agency for "hurting the feelings of basketball fans". A month later Beijing authorities fined the organisers of a small Beijing show 50,000 yuan, (around $7,700 at the time) for "using vulgar terms in its performance which violate social morality".

But the punishment of Li and XiaoGuo represents an escalation

and will definitely impact China's burgeoning stand-up comedy industry and the boundaries of making jokes both on stage and off. Whether Li's case will be judged within the legal framework is still unknown as the government seems to be weighing up the pros and cons of penalties to be meted out. How Li will be punished is therefore particularly noteworthy for those who care about freedom of speech, the rule of law and the comedy landscape in China. ✖

Qian Gong is a senior lecturer in the School of Education of Curtin University, Australia. She was a journalist at China Daily for a decade and a scholar on cultural studies and Chinese media. Jian Xu is senior lecturer in communication at Deakin University, Australia, where he co-convenes the Asian Media, Culture and Society Research Group

This is an edited version of an online article

52(02):20/22|DOI: 10.1177/03064220231183798

An Unlasting Home

MAI AL-NAKIB

A RICHLY IMAGINED SAGA SPANNING LEBANON, IRAQ, INDIA, THE UNITED STATES AND KUWAIT

Sara is a philosophy professor at Kuwait University. Her relationship with Kuwait is complicated; yet since her return from California following her mother's death, a certain inertia has kept her there.

When she is accused of blasphemy – and finds herself under threat of execution – Sara realises she must reconcile her feelings and her place in the world once and for all.

Awaiting trial, Sara retraces the past and the lives of the women who made her.

An Unlasting Home brings to life the tragedies and triumphs of three generations of Arab women. At once intimate and sweeping, it is an unforgettable family portrait and a spellbinding epic tale.

'A testament to the eternal vibrancy and pluck of women in the Arab world' *Financial Times*

£14.99 ◆ Fiction ◆ Paperback ◆ eBook available

SAQI
www.saqibooks.com

18-24 Turnham Green Terrace, London W4 1QP
T:(020) 7221 9347

Silent disco

Ahead of Zimbabwe's general election in August, **ANDREW MAMBONDIYANI** explores the worrying trend of silenced musicians

OFFICERS FROM THE Zimbabwe Republic Police violently stopped Winky D's show in Chitungwiza, a city a few kilometres outside the capital, Harare in early March. The celebrated reggae-dancehall artist, otherwise known as Wallace Chirumiko, had released an album on New Year's Eve with lyrics laying bare various social, political and economic ills bedevilling the country.

Thousands of his fans attended the album launch in Harare, but the songs have now been banned from the country's public broadcaster and other stations controlled by president Emmerson Mnangagwa's cronies.

The heavy-handed actions by the police in Chitungwiza were condemned by opposition politicians, law makers, human rights watchdogs, journalists and fellow musicians.

At the end of April, live on stage, Winky D finally spoke out: "They want to arrest the music. They must leave the music to flow like water in the river. They don't have to control my playlist. I have to play what I want – I have to play what you want."

The silencing of musicians in Zimbabwe comes ahead of the country's general election in August. Mnangagwa and his ruling party, Zanu PF, are facing a stiff challenge from the opposition Citizens Coalition for Change, a new party led by Nelson Chamisa.

Mnangagwa came to power in 2017 through a military coup that toppled long-time leader Robert Mugabe. He had promised to start with a clean slate, with a pledge to implement various reforms in the country.

Under his so-called New Dispensation, Mnangagwa had promised to bring in sweeping political, legislative, media and electoral reforms. But, six years after the coup, nothing has changed. Instead, political opponents, journalists and human rights activists have been jailed.

The persecution of musicians by the government is a recurring pattern in the country, which emerged from colonial Zimbabwe, then known as Rhodesia.

After the country gained independence in 1980, the repressive regime under Mugabe continued on a path of persecuting and silencing musicians deemed to be anti-government

Zimbabweans cannot be free if they're not united. Zimbabweans must be united

ABOVE: Winky D performing in London in 2012;
LEFT: Veteran Zimbabwean musician Thomas
Mapfumo performing in New York in July 1992

and that might affect the ordinary man's thinking about the pending elections," said Zindi, who also writes a weekly newspaper column on music and the history of music in Zimbabwe.

"The song Ibotso [on the new album] rattled the authorities and has made Winky D a marked man."

In this particular song, the singer chronicles the deteriorating socio-political and economic situations in Zimbabwe. It includes a line which translates to: "I'm just a singer, I don't have a spear, I don't have a sword."

Zindi said that the right to free expression "includes the right to hold opinions and to impart information and ideas without interference by public authority."

Zindi believes that under Mnangagwa, the country is returning to the conditions seen under former prime minister Ian Smith's colonial regime and the Mugabe era, where anyone influential who spoke out would be banned or incarcerated. He highlights the case of musician Thomas Mapfumo, nicknamed The Lion of Zimbabwe.

Before independence, Mapfumo's political music was banned from state-controlled radio by Smith's regime, and he was then imprisoned without charge for 90 days. His *chimurenga* (struggle) music was a popular genre during the fight for liberation.

In later years, Mapfumo morphed into a fierce critic of Mugabe and his government – a government that had become corrupt and an outpost of human rights violations. More than two decades ago, Mapfumo went into exile in the USA to escape being targeted by the regime. He is still there today, having also spoken out against Mnangagwa's government. When Mapfumo's brother died in 2022, he could not attend his burial in Zimbabwe for fear of reprisal.

After Winky D's show was shut down, Mapfumo spoke to his fans through a video message. He urged them to remain resolute and to continue to fight against Mnangagwa's regime.

– much to the chagrin of rights activists.

Fred Zindi, a renowned Zimbabwean musician, academic and author, told Index that what happened at Winky D's concert in Chitungwiza showed that the democratic space is closing ahead of the forthcoming election.

He said any politically-conscious popular musician singing about what is deemed to be anti-government sentiments will become an enemy, and the government will try to suppress such thinking ahead of the election.

"Judging from the attendance Winky D's concert attracted on New Year's Eve, he certainly has an influence on society,

"Zimbabweans cannot be free if they're not united. Zimbabweans must be united," Mapfumo said.

Idriss Ali Nassah, a senior Africa researcher at Human Rights Watch, also spoke out after the incident. He said shutting down Winky D's show sent a message that the authorities were willing to harass even the most popular performers for what they say.

"The Zimbabwe government needs to quickly take strong action to demonstrate that free expression will be respected, or there will be genuine concerns that upcoming elections can't be credible, free and fair," Nassah said.

Index spoke to Cucsman, a young Zimbabwean protest musician and human rights activist, who said the system had become intolerant of anything posing a threat to its power.

"The freedom of expression of an artist is heavily limited by such censorship, where the entire meaning of an artwork could be lost," he said, explaining how constraints may even force musicians to abandon particular projects altogether.

He called for new guarantees to freedom of speech, saying: "We call upon all entities and institutions to intervene and bring sanity to the music and entertainment industry." ✖

Andrew Mambondiyani is a journalist based in Zimbabwe. He has written for the BBC and Al Jazeera, amongst others

52(02):24/25|DOI:10.1177/03064220231183799

Russian security forces arrive at a meeting held by Crimean Solidarity, an unofficial association of human rights defenders, volunteers and lawyers, in Sudak, January 2018.

CREDIT: Aliona Savchuk

When the Russians came

A series of photos from inside Crimea by photographers now forbidden from the region provide a snapshot of life under Russian occupation

VLADIMIR PUTIN DOES not want you to see these images. Taken by Alina Smutko, Taras Ibragimov and Aliona Savchuk between 2014 and 2019, they document life in occupied Crimea. Some are tender and intimate; others are signs of barbarism and menace. For simply documenting life as it is, the three photo-journalists have been banned from entering occupied Crimea and Russia for 10 to 35 years.

The large-scale persecution in the Crimean Peninsula began on the first day of the occupation. Hundreds of people have since been arrested for political reasons, most of them Crimean Tatars and some journalists, while Crimeans who are out of prison live in an increasingly restricted environment. In the Spring issue of Index, leader of the Tatars Nariman Dzhelyal, himself inprisoned, likened Crimea to a concentration camp for the 21st century.

Speaking of the images, Savchuk said that they "are a small part of all the stories from the occupation that we were lucky to see, hear and broadcast.

"These stories are about people who stayed on their native land despite intimidation and threats, arrests and trials, torture and humiliation by (pro) Russian security forces. These are stories about the destroyed destinies of hundreds of families, trumped-up terrorism, persecution based on nationality, religion, and views. But they are also about love for native land and loved ones, solidarity and mutual support, faith in the victory of truth and goodness," Savchuk said.

The photos formed part of an exhibition created by the Human Rights Centre ZMINA, in cooperation with the Mission of the President of Ukraine in Crimea. This is the first time they have been published in print, with permission. ✖

52(02):26/29|DOI:10.1177/03064220231183800

Server Karametov
(left) and Ayder
Ismailov (right) in
Simferopol on the Day
of Remembrance of
Victims of Crimean
Tatar genocide,
May 2018.

CREDIT: Taras Ibragimov

Seitmamut Asanov,
son of political
prisoner Marlen
Asanov, films his father
being escorted from
a prison van to the
court for another
hearing, June 2019.

CREDIT: Taras Ibragimov

A search takes place of Crimean Tatar Yusuf Toroz's house. After the search Yusuf and his son Server were charged with possession of weapons and drugs, although the police found nothing. Server was taken away to an unknown destination.

CREDIT: Alina Smutko

Women pray at the house of the Deputy Chairman of the Mejlis, Crimean political prisoner Akhtem Chiygoz, on his birthday in Bakhchysarai, 14 December 2016. In occupied Crimea the home is often the safest place to pray.

CREDIT: Alina Smutko

Festive prayer at a mosque in honor of the release of political prisoner Enver Krosh after his sentence, February 2018.

CREDIT: Aliona Savchuk

Ibram Kashka at the grave of his mother Vedzhie, August 2018. During her life, Vedzhie was a renowned activist. Russian security forces detained her, at aged 82, on 23 November 2017. She died in detention.

CREDIT: Taras Ibragimov

The language of war and peace

Hot on the heels of his latest book, Mikhail Shishkin tells **JP O'MALLEY** how silence around
Russia's collective trauma leaves hopes for a progressive future in tatters

"THE PEOPLE WERE silent, as
Pushkin put it in the last line of this
verse tragedy," Mikhail Shishkin
explains from his home in Zurich.

He is quoting from the verse play
Boris Godunov, written by Alexander
Pushkin in 1825, which features a feeble-
minded tsar in Russia's Time of Troubles.
Although this period ended in 1613, the
situation is strikingly similar today, the
62-year-old Russian novelist insists.

"Most Russians stay silent and take
the side of the aggressor in the war in
Ukraine," he said.

Shishkin's prose has been translated
into almost 30 languages and has won
numerous international literary prizes.
His novels include Taking Izmail and

ABOVE: Shishkin's latest book, exploring Russia's
past, present and future

Maidenhair and he remains the only
author to have won Russia's three major
literary prizes: the Russian Booker Prize,
the Russian National Bestseller, and the
Big Book Prize.

In late March 2023, Shishkin
published My Russia: War or Peace? The
book reads like an extended long-form
essay and explains Russia's past, present
and future to a Western audience. The
narrative begins in February 2022,
when Vladimir Putin launched a so-
called "special military operation" in
Ukraine. The Russian president assured
his population he was going to save
Russians, Russian culture and the
Russian language from Ukrainian fascists.

Shishkin, whose mother was born in
Ukraine, points to the glaring irony: the
worst atrocities of the war so far have
been committed in Russian-speaking
cities in the east of Ukraine such as
Mariupol, where tens of thousands of
Ukrainian citizens are said to have died
at the hands of Russian forces.

"War crimes have been committed
not only against Ukrainian people but
against the Russian language, too,
which Putin has removed dignity from,"
Shishkin said.

"The language of Vladimir
Nabokov, Sergei Rachmaninoff, Leo
Tolstoy, Marina Tsvetaeva, Joseph
Brodsky and Andrei Tarkovsky has now
become the language of war criminals
and murderers."

Shishkin's book examines Russia's
centuries-long relationship with Europe,
including the mid-19th century debate
that split the country's intelligentsia into
two camps. Slavophiles claimed Russia
had always been defined by its Slav
culture and Orthodox religion – with
origins going back more than 1,000 years

to Kyivan Rus, a political federation
founded in Kyiv in the ninth century
by Viking slave traders. Westerners,
conversely, believed Russia needed to
embrace its historical links with western
Europe to progress and modernise.

That ideological argument continues
today. But since Russia has no proper
civic public forum, a debate isn't taking
place. Besides, the Slavophiles are inside
the Kremlin and most of the Westerners
continue to leave Russia.

"In Russia, you have two groups of
people who speak the same language,
share the same territory, but who
have two very different views of the
world," Shishkin told Index. "The fall
of Byzantium [in 1453] left Russia as
the only remaining independent state
governed by the Orthodox faith. Ever
since, autocracy and victory over its
enemies has been the country's sole aim."

That trend continued right up until
the 20th century. The Bolsheviks banned
religion and "thought they were saving
the world from capitalism in 1917, in
fact they merely [re-created] the Russian
empire [in a new form]".

Then "sham socialism replaced a sham
democracy" when the Russian Federation
replaced the Soviet Union in 1991, as
Shishkin put it. The writer left his native
Moscow for Switzerland not long after
that event, partly for family reasons.

"My wife, a Swiss citizen, became
pregnant in 1995 and did not want to
raise our son in Russia," he explained.

The author has lived a peripatetic
existence over the past two decades,
moving between Switzerland, the UK,
Germany and the USA. Occasionally, he
has returned to Moscow.

He moved back temporarily in 2011,
during the Snow Revolution, which

saw the biggest political protests in Russia since the fall of the Soviet Union. By February 2013, however, he could see that the Putin regime wasn't going anywhere. This inspired him to pen an open letter explaining how he would not be representing his country at BookExpo America, an international literary event in New York. His invitation had come directly from the Kremlin's Federal Agency for Press and Mass Media.

"I told them I want to represent another Russia, a free Russia," he said. Shishkin's open letter described his country's political system as akin to "a pyramid of thieves, where elections have become a farce, and courts serve the authorities".

The Kremlin responded accordingly. Shishkin was declared a Russophobe foreign agent and traitor. "It's impossible for me now to go to Russia today," he said. "I would be put in prison immediately."

It's all reminiscent of the past – during the Soviet era, Shishkin's brother, uncle and grandfather (who died in Siberia) were all locked up as political dissidents.

The author describes Russian society since the turn of the century as "a hybrid dictatorship with alternative sources of information".

Then, in February 2022, the situation drastically altered. Shishkin highlights two media institutions that refused to follow a pro-Kremlin agenda: Echo of Moscow, a liberal radio station, and TV Rain, an independent TV channel. Last year, when the war began, both were forced to halt operations inside Russia and have since moved their operations abroad, broadcasting in exile from western European cities.

Without complete de-Putinisation, Russia has no future

ABOVE: Russian writer Mikhail Shishkin, who now lives in Zurich

Shishkin said that while state television continued to brainwash most Russian citizens, it's still possible to access unbiased reliable sources of information inside Russia, via Telegram channels.

"For the Russian people it's about choosing between two truths," he said. "Imagine you are the father of a young Russian soldier who was killed in Ukraine. One truth says: Ukraine wants to build an independent state and democracy and your son is a fascist and came to kill Ukrainians. The other truth says: your son, like his grandfather, is a hero, and died defending his home country against fascists."

As for the war in Ukraine, Shishkin believes it will continue to drag on while Putin remains in the Kremlin. "That could be [for] two months or two years, nobody knows really," he said.

Once Putin goes, though, events will move quickly and chaotically, the author predicts. "Ukraine will win the war, but of course not with American tanks on Red Square in Moscow, so inside Russia there will be a struggle for power, culminating in a lawless society with a

criminal war between different gangs."

Shishkin believes that "without complete de-Putinisation, Russia has no future".

But he remains cautiously sceptical about the future of his homeland, explaining that it is inextricably linked to the collective trauma of Russian history which, crucially, most Russians don't want to honestly assess in the public domain.

"To introduce democracy in a potential new independent Russian state, we would need the critical mass of citizens," Shishkin concludes. "But in Russia today, the people who were put in charge for establishing a democratic society all come from the KGB. In Russia, we don't have citizens. We have slaves with a medieval mentality."✖

JP O'Malley is a freelance journalist based in London

52(02):30/31|DOI:10.1177/03064220231183802

Writer's block

The Hong Kong government went from rewriting history to erasing it, but the people are fighting back – with blockchain, writes **STACEY TSUI**

" I WAS SCHEDULED TO work the night shift that day, but I woke up before my alarm went off. I was immediately jolted awake by the hundreds of message notifications on my phone and I knew then that something big had happened," said Kelvin (not his real name). The former reporter at the pro-democracy online news outlet Stand News is revisiting the day the Hong Kong police raided the newsroom.

"I didn't know what to do," he told Index. "Every day, I knew what was expected of me: I had to get dressed and go to work. But at that moment I just didn't know what I was supposed to do. I couldn't go on assignments. I realised I wasn't a reporter anymore."

The sight of a newsroom filled with hundreds of police officers could make you almost forget that Hong Kong was once a bastion of press freedom – until the enactment of the National Security Law in 2020. Being widely recognised as "vaguely defined with harsh penalties", the law criminalises "conspiring to print, publish, distribute or display seditious publications", making it possible for journalism to be a crime.

Since its implementation, local news has been overrun with stories of newsroom closures, mass arrests and rampant censorship – some of which involves the pruning of old material online.

In 2021, for example, public broadcaster Radio Television Hong Kong started erasing content that was more than a year old, meaning programmes covering the 2019 Hong Kong protests were wiped from its website.

But citizens are fighting back – through blockchain technology. These blockchains are databases where the data held is immutable and unalterable. Once it is sent to a blockchain network, data cannot be deleted by the authorities. These chains have gained popularity in countries under despotic regimes, including China. In 2018, for example, a letter from a #MeToo activist was immortalised online when it was placed on a blockchain network.

In Hong Kong, the potential for this technology is growing as the city is taking a much more relaxed approach to regulating the technology than Beijing is. Tech-savvy citizens have begun backing up articles from Hong Kong tabloid Apple Daily and episodes of RTHK shows using decentralised file storage platform Arweave and LBRY, a blockchain content-sharing platform. Some have also turned to decentralised publishing (DePub) using LikeCoin, an open-source blockchain-based publishing infrastructure for content creators which aims to ensure integrity and prevent changes being made by a single entity.

"The demand to put content on blockchain is universal," said Kin Ko, one of the founding members of LikeCoin. When he first joined the team, back in 2017, he did not expect this development. His goal was to simply "support writers and conserve journalism".

"Many think the internet is free and open, but it in fact is just another walled garden," he said.

Before their closure, some Hong Kong independent news outlets

☰ News is the first ☰ draft of history

ABOVE: Staff at the Apple Daily printing facility just before it was closed, June 2021. Tech-savvy citizens have uploaded Apple Daily articles to blockchains to stop them being forever deleted

including Stand News and Citizen News also published with LikeCoin.

"With blockchain's immutability, once content is registered on blockchain we will have ownership and autonomy over our own content. It cannot be erased by a platform when it closes," said Ko.

A former columnist at Apple Daily, who wished to be referred to as Pui, began publishing with LikeCoin in 2018.

"At first, I was just glad that there was another platform to publish my

Many think the internet is free and open, but it in fact is just another walled garden

CREDIT: Jessie Pang/Reuters/Alamy

work, and the blockchain technology behind it wasn't really my focus until the closure of Apple Daily," he said.

"I never imagined that my years of hard work as a writer could go up in smoke in a split second."

Pui, who has worked full-time in the media for years, said: "News is the first draft of history. If news is removed, the piece of history will disappear. When Stand News and Apple Daily announced their cessations of operations, netizens raced to back up content.

"If we start publishing content or uploading news footage on decentralised platforms, even if certain websites are shut down in the future, history can still be preserved."

Technologists in Hong Kong are facing a new hurdle, though, with proposed legislation to regulate virtual asset exchange operators. Unlicensed providers will not be allowed to operate in Hong Kong, making the threshold for individuals to acquire cryptocurrencies higher and, in effect, making it more difficult to make blockchain decentralisation more popular.

Amid the closure of so many newsrooms, some veteran journalists have launched other online outlets. Kelvin is working for one of them – remaining a journalist, refusing to give up.

However, notwithstanding his continued pursuit of writing and the adoption of LikeCoin by the outlet he

works for, Kelvin still has to self-censor, which is frustrating. For a reporter in Hong Kong, the red line is ever-shifting.

"It's hard to know where the line is anymore," he lamented. "What we could have written about before might now be deemed illegal. And there are even topics that some outlets can cover while others can't.

"The reason I became a journalist has always been clear to me – I wanted to have the freedom to speak the truth, no matter the consequences. When I joined Stand News, I knew that it could be my last chance to fulfil that dream."

He now dreams of a future where no one will be arrested for factual reporting, no matter where they choose to publish their work.

"Even though my time at Stand News was brief, I often find myself daydreaming [that] one day Stand News would be back, and at that time I'll be an experienced journalist and will be able to use all the skills I have learned to report the truth and make a difference."

Like Kelvin, Ko still persists in the ambition of decentralisation. "We talk about decentralisation all the time, and we want to start from ourselves. It's a kind of education [and,] at the same time, a lesson for us," he said.

"Back in the day, we didn't have services like PayWave, either – until it became widely circulated. Now some would refuse to go to a store without a card machine." ✖

Stacey Tsui is a journalist from Hong Kong

52(02):32/33|DOI:10.1177/03064220231183803

The Russians risking it all

Despite the odds and the heavy punishments, resistance still exists in Russia. **KATIE DANCEY-DOWNS** talks to those who are braving it to stand up to Putin

"EVERYBODY WHO WALKS out into the street knows that they might walk straight into a prison," explained Dan Storyev, the managing editor of human rights media project OVD-Info. Despite the high risks there is what Storyev calls "an epidemic of direct action" — people are setting military recruitment offices on fire. Solitary pickets happen almost daily. Others place flowers on monuments to Ukrainian figures.

Storyev was talking to Index a year on from our special report on the war in Ukraine, which looked into the state of resistance in Russia as part of it. Armed with a central question – what has happened to the resistance since then? – the answer was depressing. The environment in which people can resist has shrunk much further. Laws introduced at the start of the war to discourage criticism of it were purposefully vague, meaning lots of people have been arrested with little to no reason given.

"They're going to find something to charge you with anyway," said Storyev.

Dissidents are forced to make apology videos (often preceded with torture) or sing the national anthem. When The Underdog pub in Moscow was raided under suspicion of sponsoring the Ukrainian army in March, one of the patrons was forced to write "Z for Russia" on the door, before nationalistic songs were blasted through speakers. People were made to sing along to the anthem or be tasered.

There is now also a fine line in Russia between who is a dissident and who is a journalist or a lawyer. The Wall Street Journal's Evan Gerschkovich was arrested in Yekaterinburg and is now in a former KGB prison.

"By throwing Evan into detention and charging him with espionage, the Russian state basically sends a signal to everybody that if you're opposing the war, you're not safe," Storyev said. Even a US passport did not protect Gerschkovich from the harsh punishments handed out to those who speak out against the war.

With many of those who took part in anti-war demonstrations early on in the war having been arrested, these demonstrations are now a rare occurrence. In August 2022, twice-poisoned journalist and opposition leader Vladimir Kara-Murza wrote in the Washington Post that Moscow's central squares were permanently occupied by riot police to stop public rallies. Today the situation differs day by day, Storyev said, adding: "The riot police [have] proved their capacity to react to things with lightning speed. They have such a technical and numerical superiority over protesters that at this point, it is not just brave but nearly suicidal to go out and protest in Russia because the response is going to be immediate and brutal."

But, as Storyev said, "Russian civil society remains defiant".

"It's been dealt a massive blow by the full-scale invasion, and by the following intensification of Putin's war on human rights. But civil society in Russia is still very much present and very much alive," he added.

When picturing Russian dissidents, people might imagine intelligentsia or scholars. Today dissidents come from all over society. They are mechanics, fire fighters and even police officers. Alexei Moskalev is one of those unexpected dissidents — he owns a small business selling pet birds, and was sentenced to two years in prison when his daughter drew an anti-war picture.

Sometimes resistance is in the small acts, making improvements to people's lives as and when people can. For example, Storyev is running a project with OVD-Info to improve conditions in prison. One person they are helping is Kara-Murza, who is currently languishing in prison for treason, gradually losing sensation in his feet as a result of the poisonings, while receiving no medical attention. OVD-Info launched a letter-writing project to keep up Kara-Murza's morale, including translating letters from English into Russian, as only Russian-language letters are allowed into the prison.

"It used to be that they would lock you up and throw away the key and no one knew what had happened to you. Now, in large part thanks to us, that's no longer the case," Storyev said, explaining how the project shines a light on human rights abuses in Russian prisons and directs the public in putting pressure on prison authorities.

Resistance is also often creative. One such example is the Kopilka Project, which translates and distributes

How could we have been living on a dragon's back and not noticed?

CREDIT: Emin Dzhafarov/Kommersant/Sipa USA

ABOVE: Alla Gutnikova, editor (centre), and Armen Aramyan, editor-in-chief of the Doxa student magazine, (right) before the announcement of the verdict in the criminal case against them on 12 April 2022 in Moscow

Russian anti-war poems. When Russian translator Maria Bloshteyn spoke about the project in Index last summer, there were more than 100 poets involved. When Bloshteyn spoke with Index again in May, along with Kopilka editor Julia Nemirovskaya, the number exceeded 300, with more than 1,000 poems penned in the Russian language. They've published an anthology, Disbelief, which contains a selection of the poems. Nemirovskaya explained that it is a collective answer to the collectiveness of the war's atrocities. One of the poets recently told her that writing these pieces is more important than life.

Over the past year, Bloshteyn has felt the weight of responsibility that the project brings, with the possibility that they are bringing the authorities' attention to poets in Russia.

"We don't know what's going to happen to the people whose works we're translating," Bloshteyn said, but she also knows that the poets must have considered the risks. "And now that they've actually taken the stab, it's my duty to make sure that their voices are heard as loudly as possible."

In terms of what exactly is happening to Russian poets, Bloshteyn said the response is wide-ranging. Poet and activist Artiom Kamardine took part in the revived "Mayakovsky readings", which happened regularly in the Soviet era until they were banned, near Moscow's statue of the renowned poet of the 1917 Russian revolution Vladimir Mayakovsky. He read poems about the war and Ukraine. He was arrested, brutalised and still awaits trial. One Kopilka poet, Maria Remizova, was accused of defamation of the Russian military forces, and when the judge found mistakes in the procedure the case was dropped.

The punishments for anti-war Russians come not just from the state, but from themselves.　　　　→

Today dissidents come from all over society. They are mechanics, fire fighters and even police officers

RIGHT: Despite the risks, people place flowers and photos on a monument of Ukrainian poet Lesya Ukrayinka in Moscow, January 2023

→ Nemirovskaya, who left Russia 35 years ago, explained how many citizens are experiencing guilt and shame, and a sense of complicity. People ask themselves how they missed the moment when Putin could have been stopped, even if many of them have joined protests. Nemirovskaya described that feeling: "How could we have been living on a dragon's back and not noticed? We used the dragon's warmth, we used its fire for our houses... are we responsible?"

This guilt is one reason the poets risk everything. Some poets use only initials or pseudonyms, fearful of their families being implicated if they are found out but others are willing to risk their lives and use their real names.

Of course a lot of the resistance happens from afar, in countries away from the reach of the KGB. Many of the poets who write for Kopilka, for example, have left Russia. The same applies to the four student journalists from Doxa, who were sentenced to two years of correctional labour for a YouTube video they posted where they said it was illegal to intimidate students for taking part in protests supporting opposition leader Alexei Navalny. All four journalists have since received humanitarian visas and are in exile in Germany, and most of the Doxa team have also left for Europe. Three of the sentenced journalists have stepped away from journalism.

Ekaterina Martynova is Doxa editor, and she told Index that her team is burnt out, working mostly in hubs across Europe and faced with challenges like

whether it is ethically sound to buy information from the black market, for example on Telegram channels. As a media organisation that deals in opinion rather than daily news, Doxa can largely avoid making this decision, but it might not be so easy for others.

She said that the understanding of what journalism actually is in Russia has changed, echoing Storyev's suggestion that there is a fine line between a dissident and a journalist — more than objective information, Martynova said people need to know what they should be doing. "During the war times, you cannot say that you are just a journalist... you should be an anti-war activist," she said.

At the end of April, a new case was launched against Doxa's social media manager, Maria Menshikova, claiming that she had called for terrorism in a social post. She is no longer in Russia,

although her parents' apartment has been targeted, Martynova explained. The majority of the Doxa team might be living outside Russia, but Martynova does not believe that anywhere is truly safe for them.

"In late November last year, another state department suggested that Doxa should be recognised as extremist," Martynova said. "The extremist label is very different from the foreign agent label. If we will be recognised as extremists, we will be the first media who will be."

Ultimately Martynova knows it would be easier to give up on journalism. For her, being a Russian journalist living outside the country is both a privilege and a responsibility. The pressure is immense for civil society actors when deciding whether to leave or stay, and what they risk when they continue to speak up. For many there appears to be little choice. They cannot remain silent. ✖

Katie Dancey-Downs is assistant editor at Index

52(02):34/36|DOI:10.1177/03064220231183804

One Kopilka poet, Maria Remizova, was accused of defamation of the Russian military forces

The 'truth' is in the tea

When a local tea house got embroiled in a free speech row, **JEMIMAH STEINFELD** investigated its links to conspiracy theorists and in so doing asked the age-old question – should free speech have limits?

ABOVE: The outside of the Tea House Theatre in Vauxhall, London. The venue has been mired by controversies in recent years

CREDIT: Simon Reynolds

N THE LEAD-UP to Christmas, when everyone in the UK was looking forward to the first restriction-free festive period in years, a London tea house decided to host an event discussing the "pandemic scam", the "World Economic Forum" and the "cancel culture mob". Before it took place, however, it was – somewhat ironically – cancelled.

The Tea House Theatre in Vauxhall, not far from where I live, had programmed an event featuring convicted antisemite Alison Chabloz. Following a public outcry and calls to boycott the venue, Chabloz was no-platformed. The venue's owner, Harry "Hal" Iggulden, said that while he was a firm believer in free speech, Holocaust denial was a "red line". He claims he didn't know of her views when she was booked, and that she was booked through an external group.

If that is true it was unfortunate oversight. Chabloz is an infamous Holocaust denier. Type her name into Google and that fact instantly comes up.

She has been convicted on two counts of sending an offensive, indecent or menacing message and on a third charge relating to a song on YouTube. The judge at one of her courtroom appearances called her "manifestly antisemitic".

At Index, I am served a daily diet of dictatorial overreach and dissident pushback, most of which happens elsewhere in the world. So when I stumbled across this story of conspiracy theorists and free speech absolutists on my doorstep, my curiosity was piqued. How did this London tea house become involved with someone such as Chabloz? And what – if anything – should be done? I started digging.

The building that is now the Tea House Theatre opened as a public house in 1886. It's situated on the edge of Vauxhall Pleasure Gardens, named because of its association with London's more lascivious crowd, which gained notoriety as the "Vanity Fair" in William

Thackeray's novel. At some stage it morphed into a strip club, owned by Denise D'Courtenay, a millionaire who was stabbed to death in the Dominican Republic in 2010. Iggulden took it over soon after and it was reborn a tea house.

As a local, I know it well. With its thick, velvet curtains, its chintzy antiques, teapots in knitted cosies and "We don't serve coffee" attitude, it's curated with such an enthusiastic nostalgia for the past that it almost seems to reject the present. I thought this was gimmicky marketing, until 2016. In the lead-up to the referendum on the UK's membership of the EU, posters supporting the Leave campaign were plastered on the tea house's windows. It was odd for the area – outside of Gibraltar, the London borough of Lambeth had the highest number of Remain voters in the UK.

After the UK voted in favour of Leave, the tea house starting selling what it called "Brexit fudge". I felt bad for the staff, whose accents suggested they →

Almost all have one thing in common – rampant antisemitism

ABOVE: A poster from inside the Tea House Theatre

→ were from continental Europe, and my husband and I jokingly referred to the venue as "Brexit Cakes".

I was also aware of a job ad it had posted addressed to "millennials", who were lambasted for being useless and spoilt. The ad appeared briefly on the Arts Council England website before being removed.

While such attitudes are in conflict with my own, there was nothing manifestly harmful or dangerous about them. They fitted more into the broader archetype of "Bisto nostalgia", a term coined by the late journalist AA Gill to describe those who longed for an idealised past that never really existed.

Then came the Chabloz incident. I was alerted to it via an online local parenting group. An email came through with the heading: "Vauxhall's Tea House Theatre hosting racists". The parents were upset – this was not the kind of neighbourhood they wanted for themselves or their children. In a group overrun with messages reviewing local schools and flogging used pushchairs, it suddenly became highly politicised.

One member described feeling "upset, petrified and embarrassed".

Through this thread, I found out that the tea house had run another controversial event. On 26 January 2020, on the eve of Holocaust Memorial Day, it hosted a fireside reading of The Doctrine of Fascism by Italian dictator Benito Mussolini, which it advertised as a "spine-tingling" and "terrifying masterpiece". Like the Chabloz event, people wanted the event cancelled. Unlike the Chabloz event, it was not. On the night, protesters encircled the building, which was manned by security guards. Inside, according to reports, the texts were read verbatim with no critical analysis. This, despite an advert from the time saying: "This is not a work for the faint-hearted, nor is it an endorsement of the doctrine. It is a topic for mature minds and will, we hope, spark a healthy debate."

There was more. The month before Chabloz was due to appear, the tea house hosted someone called Brett Redmayne-Titley, who was described on its website as being from the alternative media and who would tell the truth about Ukraine. I can't say whether he did tell the truth, but a scroll of Redmayne-Titley's Substack would suggest otherwise. One article is entitled "UK government funding Nazi regime?" A choice paragraph: "It is high time to factually challenge the British media cover-up of Ukraine's neo-Nazi connection by exposing the inconvenient truths regarding its allegiance to Nazi-inspired Ukrainian leader Stepon Bandera, the Ukrainian Right Sector, and the Azov Battalion whose swastikas are steeped in the blood from the slaughter of 14,000 eastern Ukrainians."

Both the Redmayne-Titley and Chabloz talks were organised by Let's Keep Talking, a group known for its conspiratorial views. In 2019, Hope Not Hate and Community Security Trust (CST) published a joint report following three years of investigating the group. They said they met regularly in central London to discuss conspiracy theories ranging from the faking of the 9/11 and 7/7 terrorist attacks to the Rothschilds' world domination. The list of people connected to Let's Keep Talking are on the extreme edges of society, from the left to the right, and almost all have one thing in common – rampant antisemitism.

I contacted Marc Goldberg at CST, who had worked on the report. He described Let's Keep Talking as being "as far gone as can be". As for healthy debate, he said, forget about it.

"They're not going to be talked down in their opinions. So you can't just go to them and say, 'Actually, the Earth is round', and convince them it is."

Goldberg believes the only way to handle such a group is to not work with them. "I believe in damage limitation. Not allowing more people to get sucked

Once you believe one ridiculous thing, your walls of belief get fuzzy

in. Once you believe one ridiculous thing, your walls of belief get fuzzy," he said, adding: "The longer they're given a platform, the worse."

That was certainly the approach adopted by one venue in London. When it caught wind of what Let's Keep Talking was about, it severed all ties and donated the money made from an event with the group to charity.

The tea house has taken a different approach. Today its programme lists nothing with Let's Keep Talking. Instead, at the time of checking in mid-May it is a roster of poetry readings, debates on contemporary (not controversial) issues and quirky music nights. The ties with Let's Keep Talking, though, have not been severed. Several months after the Chabloz incident, I spoke to Iggulden. I asked him if he would work with Let's Keep Talking again and he evaded the question. "My theatre is available for hire, at very reasonable rates," he responded.

This was my first proper interaction with Iggulden after reaching out several times. I had actually met him before, once, briefly at the Tea House Theatre, and he was pleasant – as indeed was his email response. I spoke to someone in my local WhatsApp group who said they (a musician) had performed at the venue and had only positive things to say. Another neighbour said their kids were at the same school as his and they'd never had a run-in.

But then, over coffee one morning with a different neighbour, I was told that they had been in the tea house last spring, on the same day as Russia's May Day, and noticed people wearing the George's Cross – a sign of a Vladimir Putin allegiance. It left a bad taste in their mouth. They haven't returned since. It raises a question: is more going on outside the official events programme, possibly without the knowledge of Iggulden?

RIGHT: A flyer found in the tea house, which lists common conspiracy theories circulating today

CREDIT: Jemimah Steinfeld

They noticed people wearing the George's Cross – a sign of a Vladimir Putin allegiance

By background, Iggulden is an actor and a writer. He runs the Holdfast Theatre Company, which was behind the Mussolini reading, and with his brother he co-wrote The Dangerous Book for Boys (2007). Aimed at children, it was a bestseller and generally well-received, although some did take issue with one chapter, which touches on the British Empire "in fairly neutral, somewhat laudatory terms", according to a reviewer. Another recently said that "much of it was too old fashionedly public school with out-of-date attitudes".

His online footprint, while sparse, provides further insight into what his views might be. His tweets, which date back to when he first joined and which we asked for comment on, are about as offensive as the algorithm will permit. On 2 January 2010, for example, he said: "Happy New Year... still hungover...got a new stage manager, her name's Roxanne...she's Greek...we'll take anyone..." A few months later, on 1 April, he wrote: "Question. do you

throw gays off a cliff or stone them in sharia law." According to the London Anti-Fascist Assembly, he also once had an image of a golliwog as his Facebook profile picture.

The Tea House Theatre is more active online and less political in tone. Its Twitter feed is essentially a roster of the menu of the day. With that, I'd expect the account to follow similar cafes and chefs. I was wrong. On 1 February this year, of the just 42 people it follows, all the usual right-wing suspects appear. To name just a few - Donald Trump, Boris Johnson, Jacob Rees-Mogg, Count Dankula, Priti Patel, Jordan Peterson. The closest I could surmise to someone who was a liberal was Carl Benjamin, who describes himself as a "sensible centrist".

When I ask Iggulden about the far-right leanings of his tea house, he is firm – no, these views do not reflect his own. "My views sort of align with the 19th-century Manchester school of laissez-faire liberalism," he said. "Defending free speech means defending the rights ➔

STOP the New Normal!
END the 'Great Reset'!
BREAK the 6 legs of New World Tyranny ('Order') being imposed by the World Economic Forum / W.H.O & servile politicians worldwide!
The World Economic Forum must be destroyed!

STOP the Virus CON!	STOP the Climate CON!	STOP the War CON!	STOP ALL Jab Programs NOW	Take-Down 5G & AI control!	Refuse Digital & Biometric ID!
Dr Mike Yeadon, former VP Pfizer: There's NO Covid Respiratory Virus IT'S A LIE to Control you Virus 'images' are figments of computer models! LetTheUkLive.com StopNewNormal.net @RealPiersCorbyn	Man-Made Climate-Change Does not Exist The 'Greenhouse-Effect' is #FakeScience NOT to control climate it's to CONTROL YOU! SaveScience-SaveOurSky! Download the facts ➡ WeatherAction.com Tgrams: #March4MoreCO2 #ULEZcantPayWontPay #StopZoningTyranny	The NATO-Russia war in Ukraine began 2014, upped 2022 is a cover for fuel+food hikes. IT'S WAR ON YOU RESPECT Democratic Self-determination of parts of Ukraine! LEAVE NATO! Tgram: #JustStopWarInUkraine	DEATH rates shot up in every country with CV JAB levels. it's a SLOW KILL through illness, blood-clots mis-carriages & infertility. Jabbed & Jab-Free UNITE! Tgram: #JabJustice	5G towers are data expressways to CONTROL YOU 5G High frequency EM radiation KILLS / injures: birds, bees, trees, plants, insects - pollinators & causes COVID-LIKE illness in YOU Tgram #TakeDown5G	STOP the 'Caste / Class' Social Credit Digi-ID Money sysyem of CONTROL to turn YOU on/off. NO Smart-meters! END AI 4ᵗʰ Industrial Revolution technocracy, Carbon footprint tracking, trans-gender-mania & on-line gagging! Keep Cash!

 THE UK Live

The Govt, servile fake opposition + fake Labour/deranged 'Far left'/XR have all Failed us! WE FIGHT for An Accountable Democratic World that puts Rights, Health, Well-Being, LIFE & open public+TV 'DEBATE' before BigPharma, BigTech, BigOil & MegaCorp profits & Diktats of the W.H.O / W.E.F New World TYRANNY. *There's No Debate in a NAZI State!* NO more Lockdowns! BREAK attacks on RIGHTS! STOP CULL of Elderly! RIGHTS! FOOD! FUEL! LAND! Tgram: @Piers_Corbyn_Stopnewnormal

Resist! Defy! Do Not...

→ of those whose speech we despise. To assume that defending another's right to speech is a form of approval of its substance is a grave error."

I ask him about the golliwog image. He doesn't deny it. "A long time ago I worked as an actor at the Edinburgh Fringe. I think at the time that Robertson's was removing the image off its jam, a street artist used

one with the tag line 'In a bit of a jam, pls give generously'. I found that funny. Over 10 years ago there was a different debate about freedom of expression. To judge art by how effectively it reinforces contemporary ethical standards is entirely to misapprehend its purpose."

Finally, I ask him if he has an agenda at the Tea House Theatrer.

"Is free speech an agenda? If so, I

have the honour of saying yes." He added: "As a small independent theatre, we love to hold debates and listen to opinions we might not agree with. No one is infallible and free speech for all is the best defence against totalitarianism."

Back in the online parents' forum, one person had written that "hate speech is not free speech". Both this comment and Iggulden's response to

me touch on a divisive topic in the free speech world. Those of us who campaign against censorship all agree that free speech is foundational to a democratic society. What we agree on less is whether there should be limits and whether, as Iggulden says, it is the best defence against totalitarianism.

Absolutists argue "no way" to limits – a little bit of censorship opens

the floodgates to a lot. Besides, it can be counterproductive. If unsavoury ideas are aired in the open, they can be challenged. If they are silenced, they don't disappear but just happen below our radar. Worse still, they might strengthen. Being banned confers an underdog or martyred status to those who are censored and adds authenticity to their narrative.

I have time for the absolutist argument. I also empathise with those advocating for some restrictions; for people to be granted freedom of expression up to the point where it breaks the law or, even before that, when it veers into hate speech. The problem is one person's definition of hate speech is different from another's. Just take China's guidelines for TikTok in which "hate speech" includes attacks on the government.

In 1992, free-speech organisation Article 19 published a report in response to these dilemmas, in which it said there were instances where the right to free expression will collide with the right to live free from persecution, and in that case the latter should win out. Except, it asked: "What evidence can be pointed to that, at least in isolation, suppression has deterred racism, intolerance and bigotry?" Here people cite the Weimar Republic, which had robust hate speech laws, as counter-example.

At the same time, Article 19's question could be flipped on its head. It could be asked "What evidence can be pointed to that no suppression has led to more bigotry?" The Tea House Theatre event with Chabloz happened just days after the artist Ye (formerly Kanye West) appeared on Infowars and declared his respect for the Nazis. In my Twitter echo-chamber he was ridiculed. Yet when I went to post my own tweet and used the hashtag "#KanyeWest", I was plunged

LEFT: Following antisemitic rants, a mural that once featured Kanye West is painted over in Chicago, October 2022

into the upside-down world: Twitter suggested the two most popular hashtags of the hour – after his name – were "#Kanyeisright" and "#Kanyewasright". I later read that following Ye's rants, spikes in violence against Jews were reported in Los Angeles.

It's fairly clear that extremist views do produce real-life consequences, even in the absence of a direct call to arms. At the same time, banning them from the public space is not necessarily the correct course. There is, sadly, no best course of action here.

As I contemplated these fault-lines, I reached out to Richard Sambrook, former director of BBC News, who was at the BBC when then far-right British National Party leader Nick Griffin was invited onto Question Time in 2009. I wanted to know if, with hindsight, he thought that was the right call.

"My view was that we would occasionally put on extreme views if it had context around it, and we challenged them. We did that with Nick Griffin," said Sambrook. He explained that it was important to acknowledge the reality that these extreme views exist.

I asked him about the fact that membership to the BNP immediately increased after the show, to which he replied: "Those elements will always exist. I don't think it will be a surprise that if you have Nick Griffin on, people in those places will get excited. The biggest question is if the greater benefit of having these views exposed outweighs the smaller price of people on the fringe? It's impossible to quantify."

Sambrook indulged my tea house interest and responded with his own take: "In a sense, it's more straightforward in a regulated environment. Broadcast is regulated. There are guardrails and a framework to work within. If you're a private place – a bookshop or a theatre – you can do what you want."

He added: "The thing about regulation is it implies responsibilities. All rights have responsibilities and ➔

→ free speech is the same. In the end, you have to provide some accountability to the organiser and there is a way to do that. [Iggulden] needs to understand there is a price to pay. If you're going to be responsible, there needs to be a sanction." In the BBC's case, said Sambrook, it's a fine by the regulator; for the tea house, it's a boycott.

Where does this leave the Tea House Theatre? Perhaps this curious story is an example of free speech actually working well. Iggulden's venue programmed Chabloz; it broke no laws in doing so, no one physically forced it to cancel the event, and the tea house remains open today. On the other side of the fence are local people increasingly uneasy about the right-wing swing of the venue. Many protested and continue to boycott the place. No one that I know of was harmed in an obvious, quantifiable way, and everyone got to express how they felt.

In the name of research, I visit the tea house after the Chabloz incident. It's the last day of February and it is bone-chilling outside. I sit next to the window, by a grandfather clock, and enjoy the classical music in the background. An older man sits nearby. He is dressed to the nines in a thick tweed suit with a curious pin attached. I sidle up to him when he heads to the counter and he tells me his badge is from the Free Speech Union, Toby Young's organisation. He says he is one of a handful of members who frequent the tea house. We have an animated chat and he tells me how he identifies as right-wing and conservative but does not agree with all right-wing views and certainly holds fast to the notion they should be challenged. He speaks Russian but in the early part of the war he sent money to Ukraine. He travels across London to come to the tea house. He

ABOVE: A leaflet advertising the upcoming events of the tea house

describes it as a home away from home.

Our conversation wraps up and I go to the bathroom. On one of the walls is a picture of Judith Kerr's book The Tiger Who Came to Tea. The words have been changed to "The Tiger Who Ignored the Government Rules and Came to Tea" – a clearly provocative knock at the state-imposed Covid-19 lockdowns. Except, on this poster the last three words are scribbled over and in their place is "[The Tiger Who Ignored the Government Rules and] Killed People by Being Selfish". The poster – now sullied – could have been taken down. Instead, it remains, view and counter-view on display.

On the way out, I spy a table of pamphlets. There, amongst ones advertising upcoming events, is a hectic flyer reading "STOP the New Normal!" It's from an organisation called Let the UK Live and outlines across two sides of A5 all the current cliché conspiracy theories, from man-made climate change being a myth to 5G towers

being data expressways to control us. I'm certain the tea house has become a sort of unofficial HQ for London's conspiracy theorists, whether Iggulden has encouraged this or not.

As I leave the Tea House Theatre, I think about BBC journalist Marianna Spring's podcast Death by Conspiracy – the real-life story of a man in the UK who died from Covid after falling into a conspiracy hole that said the pandemic was a hoax. It happened in Salisbury, which is a quaint city, unassuming, a bit like a tea house. Gary Matthews, the victim, heard "pandemic scam" views similar to the ones circulating at Iggulden's venue, and likely died because of them. Both examples remind me of the duty we supporters of free speech hold: to ensure people aren't punished for what they say and equally to ensure people aren't punished for what they hear – and to know where to draw the line. ✖

≡ He is dressed to the nines in a thick tweed suit with a curious pin attached

Jemimah Steinfeld is editor-in-chief of Index

52(02):37/42|DOI:10.1177/03064220231183807

Waiting for China's tap on the shoulder

CHU YANG describes how China's long arm is reaching into her European sanctuary

T HAS BEEN almost three years since I left China and I still sometimes have nightmares.

In my dreams I'm always on the run, although most of the time I can't tell what's chasing me. There is one I remember vividly. I stood on top of a mountain and saw floods covering the valley and lowlands, and then started running in the opposite direction.

This dream perhaps reflected the deep insecurity and frustration that I still feel after three years of living in Europe. When Covid-19 first broke out in Wuhan, I was among the early sources that alerted the public about an upcoming pandemic. Then, unexpectedly, my Weibo account was suspended and my new account on Douban (a Chinese database and social networking site) was targeted for censorship, making posting Covid-related content almost impossible.

The suffocation of being silenced drove me to start a Telegram channel to archive censored content on Chinese social media. After learning what happened to other organisers of similar projects, either "drinking tea" with police and security officers or being arrested, I decided to leave for Europe out of safety concerns.

But, for me, Europe is not a safe haven, either. I am always reminded of the shadow that I was running from. Some of my insights have been useful to European institutions in understanding China's digital landscape, but some of my writing has had to go unattributed. Last year I worked for an organisation, where my work had to remain completely anonymous. This is, of course, for my own safety, but it also means that I have to partially sacrifice my career advancement in order to preserve myself. Even here it is not easy for me to live fully or express myself without fear.

I could certainly have chosen to be more outspoken, but it might have come at a huge cost. Some fellow journalists have been subjected to public shaming and doxxing by "patriotic" bloggers, one of the most notorious perpetrators being Bu Yi Dao (which translates as "Add One More Stab"), who targets Chinese journalists and researchers working overseas. Worse still, family and friends can be used as weapons against you.

One of the most notable cases is that of journalist Vicky Xiuzhong Xu, whose harassment and public shaming reached a peak after her role in an Australian Strategic Policy Institute report on human rights violations in Xinjiang, published in 2020. Her family, who she describes as "mainstream and conventional", has been harassed.

When I asked her about her family, she said: "They think what I'm doing is absurd and shameful. I've heard that they are also being treated poorly and ostracised in the local community because of me, and their lives are being affected in many ways. The elders do not allow my family to contact me anymore and the relationship was cut off."

This is the dilemma many journalists and researchers who live outside China face. There is no complete escape from the reach of China's long arm and many have to accept a compromised life – partially sacrificing career development and revealing minimal details about their work to their families.

With China increasingly like a black box with a tight hold on the flow of information, Chinese employees' knowledge can be an asset to organisations outside the country – but it is vital to provide them with material and emotional support. As one of those people, I hope my nightmares of running away will one day stop. But I am not sure if that day will come. ✖

Chu Yang is a journalist based in Europe

52(02):43/43|DOI:10.1177/03064220231183808

CREDIT: Share America/D Thompson

When the old fox walks the tightrope

Uganda's Anti-Homosexuality Act is a poisoned chalice – and not just for the nation's LGBTQ+ community. **DANSON KAHYANA** discusses the Act with **STELLA NYANZI**

TO A CHORUS of outrage at the end of May, Uganda's President Yoweri Museveni signed the Anti-Homosexual Bill into law, which can apply the death penalty.

When Museveni returned the bill to parliament for "strengthening" soon after it had been passed in March, it was clear that the old fox who has ruled Uganda since 1986 with an iron hand and "pretensions to the trapping of democracy" – as political scientist Aili Mari Tripp calls it – was in a fix.

On the one hand, his populist self loves the passion that the framing of homosexuality as a Western import and a corrupter of African morality arouses, so signing the bill into law gives him a new lease of political life.

Styling himself as the champion of African values, Museveni believes norms and morals can easily translate into political support at the next presidential and parliamentary elections in 2026, given the influential groups in support of the bill (the Muslim fraternity, some Christian denominations and traditionalists). This support is priceless, considering the populace's increasing anger at his regime, which has received unflattering labels including an "empty autocracy" (Yusuf Serunkuma) and "vampire state" (Allan Tacca).

On the other hand, the regime survives partly (if not mostly) because of the economic and political support it receives from Western governments such as those in the USA, Canada and some in the European Union.

These "partners" have, over the decades, closed one eye to his political excesses (rigging elections and brutalising members of opposition political parties, for example) and bankrolled him in different ways – the most obvious ones being budget support and providing large sums of money to enable Uganda's participation in continental and regional missions. Signing the bill into law could spell doom for his hold on power, since these Western governments have warned of political and economic consequences, which the USA has already made good on by revoking the visa of Anita Among, Uganda's speaker of parliament.

This is the tightrope he had to walk – but not for the first time. He did the same in 2014 when he signed the 2013 Anti-Homosexuality Bill into law. That time, what saved him from serious reprisals from the West was the Uganda Constitutional Court which, later that year, quashed the law on technical grounds. (It had been passed in parliament without the required quorum, thereby rendering it null and void). His saving grace now could be a petition from 11 activists, including lecturers, journalists and an MP, to block the implementation of the law.

Before May's developments, I asked Dr Stella Nyanzi, Uganda's leading and celebrated researcher on sexualities, what was new with this 2023 bill compared with the bill of 2013, and she said that as far as she was concerned there was nothing substantially new.

Both bills were enacted in the spirit of criminalising sexualities that were considered alien and wayward in order to protect so-called African values – a claim that is absurd given that it is colonial in origin.

"Before colonialism," Nyanzi told Index, "Africa embraced different sexualities like polygyny, polygamy and polyandry, to mention but a few. The view that Africa has always had one form of sexuality is ahistorical and a figment of the imagination."

There is something new, however.

"While the 2013 Anti-Homosexuality Bill was proposed by a Pentecostal Christian with very strong support from the US Evangelical churches, this time round the proposer of the bill is a Muslim man, with a strong backing of the Islamic faith in Uganda," she said. "He is a Member of Parliament who belongs to an opposition political party, unlike the proposer of the 2013 bill who belonged (and still belongs) to the ruling party."

Besides the pretensions to African morality that motivated this act, there is a more serious threat at stake – the government's desire to have total control over the bodies of its citizens.

Nyanzi said: "For this reason, the bill should be seen in the context of

---

≡ Styling himself as the champion of African values, Museveni believes norms and morals can translate into political support other repressive laws that the Museveni regime has passed – for instance, the Public Order Management Act (2013), the Computer Misuse Act (2011), the Anti-Pornography Act (2014), the Non-Governmental Organisations Act (2016) and the Computer Misuse (Amendment) Act (2022), among others.

"The Anti-Homosexuality Bill should be seen in the spirit of all the above laws – criminalising dissent, even in sexual matters."

Even before it was signed into law, the bill sent tremors through Uganda.

Some people fled the country, as evidenced by what is happening at welcome centres in Kenya and South Africa, to mention just two countries.

"[It] will have far-reaching effects," Nyanzi warned.

"It will be criminal, for instance, to offer certain kinds of sex education, provide certain kinds of medical services, report certain kinds of news, write certain kinds of scholarly work or works of fiction, produce certain

Both bills were enacted in the spirit of criminalising sexualities that were considered alien and wayward

kinds of movies, make certain kinds of speeches, and to rent your premises to – or even employ – certain kinds of people, because you could be accused of promoting homosexuality, and therefore contravening Section 14 of the bill."

This means that the law will not only stifle the lives and work of the people who identify as homosexual but also affect the lives and work of all Ugandans.

Even the very people who pushed for the legislation will not be safe. A religious leader could, for instance, be dragged to court for having someone who identifies as homosexual enter his or her church or mosque for prayers or for a service.

After the bill passed in parliament, Museveni found himself in a dilemma. If he did not sign it into law he would have risked alienating the pretentious, self-righteous, politically powerful Christian, Muslim and other morality crusaders who were pushing for the legislation.

And by passing it, he could at last be losing the support of his beloved

Western partners who have stuck with him even as he brutalised Ugandans who do not toe his line.

And in the time before the bill became law, he might have been facing another challenge in the background.

"The people at the helm of Uganda's parliament – [speaker] Anita Annet Among and her deputy, Thomas Tayeebwa – might want to assert their independence from the executive arm of government in a move aimed to show how powerful they are. So, while President Museveni is known to control what happens in parliament because his party has an overwhelming majority there, this time round he might find it hard to have his way to the letter."

But this being the skilled manipulator that he is, I believe that we should not underestimate him: he could still have his cake and eat it.

How? He signed it into law and waited for others to petition the Constitutional Court, as has been done by the group of 11 activists, so that the judiciary pronounces itself on the constitutionality of the new law. If the court upholds it, he will say he has nothing to do because his regime is law-abiding.

However, if the court annuls it in its entirety (as it did in 2014) or some sections of it, the West will be satisfied, to a certain degree, that Uganda's courts have a modicum of independence.

Museveni will be in his usual element. He will have survived yet another dilemma. ✖

Danson Kahyana is a Ugandan poet, scholar and author of children's literature and the outgoing president of PEN Uganda

BELOW: People appear in court in Kampala, Uganda after they were arrested in an LGBTQ+ friendly bar in 2019. They were charged with "common nuisance" but rights activists believe it was intimidation towards the LGBTQ+ community

52(02):44/45|DOI:10.1177/03064220231183809

CREDIT: Abaca Press / Alamy

Would the media lie to you?

Uncovering the truth in Afghanistan's constricted media landscape is more difficult but equally more important than ever. **ALI LATIFI** reports from Kabul

N THE NEARLY two years since the Taliban returned to power, Afghanistan has become the subject of increasingly dubious news reports, unproven claims and generalisations that have left the country's citizens trying to discern fact from fiction.

Afghanistan is ripe for the growth of inaccurate information. Restrictions on the media are increasing, there's a lack of access to information and hundreds of local media outlets are being closed due to tightening limitations on free speech and cutbacks on foreign funding. Thousands of Afghan media workers fled the country when the Taliban arrived in Kabul in 2021, as Index has reported on, and there are personal biases to consider – many people are unhappy with the Islamic Emirate's return to power.

Haroun Rahimi, an Afghan academic and author currently based in the USA, said he regularly came across both disinformation and misinformation from all sides – online and in-person.

Since August 2021, Rahimi and others have repeatedly pointed to

ABOVE: A Taliban member celebrates the year anniversary of the Taliban takeover of Afghanistan in front of the US Embassy in Kabul on 15 August 2022

examples of incorrect or misleading reporting from major international media outlets and new Afghan outfits based abroad.

One high-profile example comes from The New York Times. A year before the Taliban actually banned women from higher education, it published a story claiming that women would not be allowed into Kabul University based on a tweet from someone claiming to be the university's chancellor. The paper eventually had to issue a lengthy correction, saying it had believed the tweets to be genuine and that government officials had not replied to its requests for comment.

In a report about a young man in Kabul who had been tortured and killed by the Taliban for being gay, The Guardian used a picture of Safiullah Ahmadi. Ahmadi was very much alive and posted a video online, threatening to sue the British paper and saying nothing about the report was true. And The Washington Post had to issue a correction to a story which claimed the Taliban had voided thousands of divorces for Afghan women after it was called out for inaccuracies.

Rahimi said that although fake news and disinformation were global problems, Afghanistan has been especially affected since the fall of the Western-backed Islamic Republic.

During the 20-year Western occupation of the country, Afghanistan's press freedom ranking increased. Although it was still ranked by the Reporters Without Borders Press Freedom Index as 128th out of 179 countries, in 2013 the country outranked many others in the region – including Iran, Pakistan and Turkmenistan. However, since the Taliban took over there have been frequent reports of journalists being detained, beaten and tortured by the authorities.

A shrinking media space has created a situation where bias and unsubstantiated claims permeate social and traditional media, Rahimi explained. He said pro-Islamic Emirate groups "highlight successes and try to downplay the shortcomings and failures" of the Taliban-led government, while those who oppose them try to "build the narrative that everything is going horribly wrong in the country".

Rahimi said both sides unquestioningly promoted and spread stories that fitted their respective narratives without making the effort to verify their validity.

Michael Kugelman, the South Asia Institute director at the US-based Wilson Centre, picked up on the dangers of this trend in a tweet, writing: "Lots of mis-info is floating around social media on the Taliban. Much of it accuses the group of doing bad things it hasn't actually

Some news consumers, once aware of this misinfo, shrug off all the reports on Taliban brutalities that ARE true

done. This runs the risk of making some news consumers, once aware of this mis-info, shrug off all the reports on Taliban brutalities that ARE true."

Rahimi said he tended to ignore fake news and misinformation to avoid drawing more attention to it. However, even when he does point out factual inaccuracies, it does little to change people's minds.

"The sentiment doesn't go away … The 'emotional truth' is still there," he said.

When it comes to major international media outlets misreporting, Rahimi said he was disappointed but not surprised. Greater numbers of foreign journalists are either being barred from the country or facing greater difficulties obtaining press visas, meaning few have an on-the-ground presence. This creates a situation where journalists who lack a deep knowledge of Afghanistan are being assigned to the country. They are more susceptible to intermediaries and sources who, according to Rahimi, often have "a very coloured vision of the country".

Rachel Pulfer is the executive director at Journalists for Human Rights, an organisation that aims to strengthen human rights reporting. She said ongoing cutbacks and layoffs across the media industry made it more difficult for outlets to properly vet every story – especially in countries such as Afghanistan.

"Often, fact-checking is the first thing to be cut," she said, calling disinformation "the issue of our time" and insisting that journalists should be given the right tools to uncover false reports.

Pulfer explained that those who traded in disinformation specifically sought out "divisive issues" and searched for things that "seem just believable enough" to base their

campaigns or stories around.

For Saad Mohseni, the CEO of Afghanistan's largest private media network, the Moby Group, the current situation has forced his cadre of journalists to be extra diligent about what they report.

"Our journalists in the country go to great lengths not to run a story until it's verified," he said.

Because Moby staff still live in Afghanistan, they know that the cost of reporting false or unproven news can be extremely high.

The Committee to Protect Journalists said intelligence officials were a growing threat to free media in the country, with several journalists reporting that they had been arrested and interrogated.

Mohseni agreed that there was no shortage of people who deliberately spread false narratives.

"Today's reality is probably unacceptable for many of them, so these people create things that suit their agendas," he said.

He added that local and international journalists must take biases into account when they vet their sources. With discussions around Afghanistan becoming so polarised, he said the trend of misleading information was exacerbating the problem of people being trapped in ideological bubbles.

Mohseni believes they can "no longer make a distinction between reality and what their version of the truth may be".

At a time when more than 28 million Afghans require humanitarian and protection assistance, accurate information is vital. ✖

Ali Latifi is a journalist based in Afghanistan

52(02):46/47|DOI:10.1177/03064220231183816

Britain's Holocaust island

The peaceful island of Alderney was involved in the darkest chapter of World War II. Both residents and politicians have tried to keep a lid on this history but, as **MARTIN BRIGHT** highlights, the silence is ending

LEFT: The entrance gates to Lager Borkum today, one of the labour camps on the island of Alderney during the German occupation

I N A WEST London art gallery, a pock-marked relief sculpture provides a devastating visual representation of a wartime Nazi atrocity. The piece is both a work of art and evidence from a crime scene: a cast of a wall riddled with bullet holes. The cast could have been taken from any number of sites across Nazi-occupied Europe. But this wall is on Alderney – one of the Channel Islands and part of the British Isles – which surrendered to the German army in 1940.

The artist Piers Secunda, who created the work, has been told by forensics experts that it was used by a German firing squad. Secunda is part of a growing group of campaigners, journalists, researchers and politicians who believe the full story of the occupation of Alderney has never been told. In particular, he believes the fate of Jewish prisoners on the island has been conveniently minimised to protect the idea of British exceptionalism. If he is right, we will have to reassess our understanding of the history of the geographical boundaries of Hitler's Final Solution. Hence the exhibition's title: The Holocaust on British Soil.

Just eight Jews are officially recorded as dying on Alderney. Secunda, who describes himself as a researcher as well as an artist, is sceptical. Another of his works includes reproductions of lists of deportees compiled by the French Nazi-hunter Serge Klarsfeld. Secunda is now writing to the families of 400 French Jews who are known to have been transported to the island from the notorious transit camp at Drancy in the suburbs of Paris.

"If many hundreds of Jews were sent to Alderney and we know the death rate of prisoners was high – between 30% and 40% – how is it possible that only eight people died on the island? There is a disconnect, and my interest is to join the dots," he told Index.

While Alderney is technically a Crown Dependency and not a part of the United Kingdom, the British government was responsible for the surrender of the Channel Islands. The occupation of these islands has always been an inconvenient truth. By the summer of 1940, Prime Minister Winston Churchill's War Cabinet concluded the islands could not be defended, and at the beginning of July, Jersey, Guernsey, Sark and Alderney were all occupied. However, unlike on the other islands, all but a handful of people on Alderney were evacuated. This paved the way for the island to be turned into a vast prison for slave workers constructing Hitler's sea defences. In January 1942, therefore, four camps – Helgoland, Norderney, Sylt and Borkum – were set up for workers from so-called Operation Todt. Conventional wisdom is that the majority of those transported to the island were Russian prisoners of war. But the records show a significant proportion of those in the camps were Spanish Republicans, north African Arabs and French Jews.

The conditions on Alderney were appalling and, in common with other Nazi work camps, prisoners were beaten and starved. Many succumbed to disease. Those who could no longer work were sent to camps in mainland Europe where they were murdered. The overall numbers of those who died on the island is also the subject of academic controversy: the minimum estimate is between 700 and 1,000 people, but experts believe the actual figure could be much higher.

Immediately after the liberation of Alderney, two senior British soldiers, Major Cotton and Major Haddock, were sent to investigate war crimes. As a result, the Judge Advocate General's (JAG) office, the body responsible for bringing Nazis to justice, concluded the conditions were akin to those in other concentration camps in German-occupied territory: "The position here is somewhat similar to Belsen, stronger perhaps because the offences were committed on British territory." A young captain, Theodore Pantcheff, was brought in to carry out a full investigation. In September 1945 he wrote: "Wicked and merciless crimes were carried out on British soil in the last three years." →

Britain did not bring a single German officer to justice for what happened on Alderney

→ And yet Britain did not bring a single German officer to justice for what happened on Alderney. Instead, the authorities chose to focus on the Russian victims of the regime in the island's camps and shift the responsibility for any investigation to the Soviet authorities. In October 1945, Pantcheff's report was sent to Moscow, where it lay in the archives until 1993. The British copy was destroyed.

When the report finally came to light, it revealed that 15 suspected war criminals had been in British custody at the end of the war. In his memoirs, Pantcheff claimed that three of the most notorious of these, Maximilian List, Kurt Klebeck and Carl Hoffman, had not survived the war. This was untrue. Hauptsturmführer List was in charge of Sylt, the only SS camp on British territory. After the war, he was traced to a British prisoner-of-war camp and was said to have been handed over to the Russians. In fact, he was living in Germany well into the 1970s. Obersturmführer Klebeck, List's deputy, lived out his days in Hamburg, despite being convicted of other war crimes in 1947 and being the subject of German investigations in the 1960s and the 1990s. Most shocking is the story of Major Hoffman, the Kommandant of Alderney and its four camps, who Pantcheff said had been handed over to the Russians and executed in Kyiv in 1945. The British government was forced to admit the truth in 1983: that Hoffman was taken from Alderney and held in the London Cage – for prisoners of war – until 1948, when he was released and allowed to return to Germany. He died peacefully in his bed in Hamelin, West Germany, in March 1974.

The story of Alderney is one of silence, state censorship and missed opportunities. Hoffman and the other war criminals should have faced justice immediately after the end of hostilities. The British government has never explained why it allowed them to go free nor why it pursued a policy of "Russification" of the atrocities committed on the island. But there is no doubt this was a conscious policy. The details are contained in Madeleine Bunting's 1995 book, The Model Occupation. In it she said that Brigadier Shapcott from JAG wrote in 1945 that all the inmates on Alderney were Russian, and Britain's Foreign Office concluded that "for practical purposes Russians may be considered to be the only occupants of these camps". JAG also told the Foreign Office: "No atrocities were committed against the French Jews. On balance they were treated better than the others working for the Germans."

There have been a number of attempts to correct the historical record by drawing attention to the camps on Alderney and the presence of Jewish prisoners. Most notable is the work of Jewish South African archaeologist Solomon H Steckoll, whose book The Alderney Death Camp was published in 1982 and serialised in The Observer newspaper. His direct, impassioned approach is captured in the cover blurb: "In 1943 the SS built a concentration camp on the British island of Alderney. Prisoners were worked as slaves, beaten, starved, hanged, garrotted, hurled from cliff-tops, even buried alive in setting concrete. Why have these horrific acts been kept from the public for so long?"

The Alderney Death Camp is a remarkable piece of investigative journalism driven by the author's own burning sense of injustice. Many on Alderney dismissed it as a tabloid hatchet job. But it is nothing of the kind, not least because Steckoll made it his personal mission to find Hoffman and reveal the full scale of the British government's cover-up. This will be his legacy.

Steckoll's revelations prompted a grudging recognition from the British government that it had not told the truth about Hoffman. It did not, though, lead to full disclosure. Those files on the Channel Islands that had not been destroyed remained closed for at least another decade, when Labour MP David Winnick, who is Jewish, began campaigning for their release. From May 1992, Winnick also pushed for an investigation into the war crimes on Alderney committed by Klebeck, who was by then known to be at large in Hamburg. By the end of the year, he had succeeded on both fronts (although no files released made any reference to Alderney). Winnick's campaign was followed two years later by the publication of Bunting's book. Nearly 30 years on it still bears scrutiny as a major piece of journalism; Bunting's tone as she grapples with the British government's decision-making is a mixture of shock and justified anger.

Her conclusion is stark: "Trials on British soil would have been an acutely embarrassing reminder to the British public of several painful facts about the war which the government wanted quickly forgotten: that British territory had been occupied for five years; that British subjects had collaborated and worked for the Germans on Alderney; and that Nazi atrocities, including the establishment of an SS concentration camp, had occurred on British soil."

One block on transparency has been the attitudes on Alderney itself. Academics and journalists have faced hostility on the island. Caroline Sturdy Colls, professor of conflict archaeology at Staffordshire University, was the first to apply modern forensic techniques to sites on Alderney. Her book,

CREDIT: Paul Quezada-Neiman / Alamy

LEFT: Artist Piers Secunda beside a mould of part of the execution wall from the original in Alderney, at his Alderney: The Holocaust in British Soil exhibition at Cromwell Place, London in March 2023

Adolf Island: The Nazi Occupation of Alderney, was published last year. Nearly 80 years after the end of the war, the subject of what really happened on Alderney remains highly sensitive among some residents who don't want their island paradise to become part of what they see as the Holocaust industry.

"There are certainly some islanders who want to help memorialise the victims and tell their stories, so not everyone wants to forget," Sturdy Colls told Index. "Those that do often provide reasons like not wanting the island to be tarnished by this dark history or not wanting tourism based on Nazi sites."

The archaeologist said there were a host of other reasons why the subject of the camps on Alderney has proved controversial. "There are many people who still don't recognise the crimes that were perpetrated as being part of the Nazi programme of persecution and/or the Holocaust. After the war, there was a conscious effort by the government

to play down the atrocities that were carried out, and so a sanitised narrative emerged that a good proportion of the British public believed or chose to believe. Some of the islanders who went back to Alderney found it too painful to discuss what had happened there, whilst some residents after the war didn't (and still don't) want the island to be known for the occupation-era sites that exist there."

There have been several key moments when a full and accurate narrative should have been told. Immediately after the war, the Pantcheff report could have led to a war crimes trial, but the British government chose to draw a veil over the atrocities. The extraordinary work of Steckoll in 1982 could have prompted an inquiry, but instead it was dismissed

as sensationalist. The combined efforts of Winnick in parliament and Bunting in the press could have opened the door in the mid-1990s, but again the government chose obfuscation rather than openness.

We have another such opportunity now. The mantle of Steckoll has been taken up by another Jewish investigator, Marcus Roberts, who is determined to pursue the truth about the Holocaust on British soil. He believes it is possible that between 15,000 and 30,000 people died on the island, with at least 1,000 being Jewish.

Roberts is the founder of the Jewish heritage charity JTrails. He began researching the Nazi camps of northern France in 2007. Two years later he turned his attention to the Channel Islands. He has been pushing for official recognition of Alderney as a Holocaust site, the establishment of an appropriate memorial and protection of Jewish graves. Roberts has established it was not just French Jews who were sent to Alderney; there were Jews from many from other parts of Europe and north Africa. His research demonstrates that a considerable number of Jews are likely to have died on the island from dysentery and disease. His view is that the push for a Soviet inquiry was a smokescreen. Roberts told The Observer: "The way I read it is that the investigation regarding the Russians was undertaken first as a diversion from war crimes against other nationalities, but also there was definitely discussion in the papers we can read that they wanted →

In common with other Nazi work camps, prisoners were beaten and starved

One block on transparency has been the attitudes on Alderney itself

→ to guarantee access to Allied war graves on Russian territory. It was also about plausible deniability."

Although she has challenged the numbers cited by Roberts, Sturdy Colls also believes the scale of the Jewish atrocities has been downplayed. "It is evident from the wide range of testimonies available and from the surveys we did of the camps in which Jews were housed that they were treated appallingly, and more Jews likely died than we know of," she said. "The conditions in which Jews were housed were an extension of those that they were kept in elsewhere in Europe. The camps on Alderney were part of a network of sites that housed Jews and harsh punishments, terrible working and living conditions, and torture characterised their lives on Alderney."

She added that it was important to recognise the atrocities committed against other groups on Alderney – eastern Europeans and Jehovah's Witnesses, for example. "Overall, the suffering of most of the people who were sent to Alderney and were under the control of Organisation Todt and the SS has been underplayed."

The momentum towards full disclosure may now be irresistible. In recent years, investigative journalists around the world have turned their attention to Alderney, and the story has been covered by The Sunday Times and ITV in the UK, Channel 9 in Australia, Der Spiegel in Germany and The Times of India. One of the most comprehensive investigations was carried out last year by Isobel Cockerell for the international online publication Coda Story. Her article on Alderney has been nominated for the 2023 Orwell Prize for Journalism. In it she asks the key questions: "Why did the British government let evidence of German war

crimes on its soil ... remain in obscurity? Why was no one prosecuted?" She says the islanders have a range of answers: collective shame at surrendering the islands and subsequent collaboration; the post-war focus on rebuilding the country; a view that the scale of the atrocities didn't merit war crimes trials; and also that "no government wanted talk of Jewish murders on its soil".

Events in the next few years may force the government's hand and prompt ministers to correct the historical record. In 2024, the UK will take its turn as chair of the International Holocaust Remembrance Association. The body is responsible for Holocaust education, remembrance and research around the world. Lord Pickles is the UK's special envoy for Post-Holocaust Issues and the head of the UK's IHRA delegation. On visits to Alderney, Pickles has told islanders they need to come to terms with the troubled history of the camps and find a way of marking what happened with a respectful memorial.

Later this year, Pickles will announce an expert review of the numbers who died on Alderney and invite submissions from academics, researchers and members of the public. The IHRA is seeking to adopt a charter to safeguard all sites of the Holocaust in Europe. Gilly Carr, associate professor in archaeology at Cambridge University and chair of the IHRA Safeguarding Sites project, told Index: "Such sites play a crucial role in educating current and future generations about the Holocaust and help us reflect on its consequences. In this charter we take a broad approach to what we consider to be a site of the Holocaust. Jews were held in camps in Alderney and we consider these to be Holocaust sites."

Carr, like Sturdy Colls, believes the full story of Nazi atrocities has been

downplayed in the past. "Certainly, the subject of victims of Nazism in the Channel Islands as a whole, a category within which I would include Jews, political prisoners and forced labourers, has come late to the table," she said. "Because there were no war crimes trials resulting from the occupation of the Channel Islands, it became a 'non-subject' for many people."

Carr has helped develop the concept of "taboo heritage", where the legacy of war is so sensitive that people become resistant to the idea of full remembrance.

"Taboo heritage can become heritage in the end if it receives political support, but this usually takes a lot of time and investment by stakeholders," she said.

Pickles is also co-chair of the UK Holocaust Memorial Foundation, the body responsible for planning a Holocaust Memorial and Learning Centre, which will be built in sight of the Houses of Parliament. British exceptionalism will be at the heart of the new memorial. It will celebrate the Kindertransport, the scheme to rescue 10,000 children from Nazi Germany in the nine months before the outbreak of war. It will also celebrate British heroes of the Holocaust, such as Sir Nicholas Winton, who helped rescue 669 children from Czechoslovakia on the eve of war.

There is now a commitment to putting the occupation of the Channel Islands at the heart of the memorial. But what happened here does not sit easily with this narrative of exceptionalism. The horrors of Alderney are a blot on Britain's reputation, which is perhaps why the full story has been suppressed for so long. The slogan chosen for the memorial is "Confronting Evil, Assuming Responsibility". Will we now confront the evil of the camps on Alderney and assume responsibility for covering up what happened there? ✖

Martin Bright is editor-at-large at Index

52(02):48/52|DOI:10.1177/03064220231183817

CREDIT: STR/Vietnam News Agency

ABOVE: An activist (Trinh Ba Phuong) appears in court on December 2021, after being jailed for a Facebook post about a land dispute clash that left four people dead in 2020

The thorn in Vietnam's civil society side

NGOs play a fundamental role in Vietnam, but as **THIỆN VIỆT** reports, the government doesn't like them – and lets that be known

THERE WAS A reason that a movie screening in Vietnam supporting the International Day in Support of Victims of Torture was held a month earlier than it should have been. The official day wouldn't happen until 26 June, but the film screening took place in May. It's the same reason that there were no public announcements about the screening. Running the event a month early, and keeping it under the radar, helped the Hanoi-based NGO behind the event avoid scrutiny – and ultimately censorship. Nguyễn Thị Linh Huyền accompanied a close friend to the screening. She knew about it only through another friend who was personally connected to the organising team, and went to find out more. She said the gathering was an insightful and intimate occasion, where around a dozen college students and young professionals engaged in a discussion from both domestic and international perspectives.

Interested to know why the event was not shared more widely, Nguyễn approached one of the members of the organising team. She was told that if the event were publicly announced the team would have to ask for permission from local authorities, since it was foreign-funded.

"Obtaining a permit for this film screening would be impossible," said Nguyễn Vân-Anh, head of the organising team, especially during this "sensitive time". This was a reference to the recent clampdown on the non-profit sector that has led to the closure of many NGOs and the arrests of their leaders and activists across the country.

By not applying for such a permit, the organisers were taking a substantial risk. The topic of the chosen movie, torture, is delicate. Vietnam ratified ➜

→ the United Nations Convention against Torture and Other Cruel, Inhuman or Degrading Treatment or Punishment in 2015, yet has not been active in translating this commitment into practice. The country has a track record of torturing prisoners of conscience, and torture while in police custody is not uncommon. According to Nguyễn Vân-Anh, many public events in Hanoi discussing torture or the death penalty have been cancelled for "mysterious" reasons during the past decade.

Vietnamese civil society organisations, much like Nguyễn's organisation, must navigate the difficult task of promoting democratisation initiatives that receive backing from foreign entities while still complying with the unwritten rules and regulations set out by the Communist Party of Vietnam.

In addition to formally registered organisations there are informal and independent actors who are either unwilling or unable to register. Yet staying informal is by no means impervious to top-down interference. Unlike state-affiliated non-profit organisations that shy away from criticising the communist government or condemning human rights violations, independent activists, journalists and bloggers have openly exposed corruption and persecution, which makes them subject to constant harassment and crackdowns.

One of the people who has felt this pressure is Nguyễn Duy Cường, based in Ho Chi Minh City, who received funding from various foreign embassies to organise tutoring events for students from underprivileged backgrounds. He said that he had to meet with local police periodically to report this work.

"Even though police officers attend my every single tutoring session and see that my activities are harmless, they still 'invite me for tea' every now and then," he said.

The communist government, which seized power in 1945, touts its "socialist rule of law" and claims to be a state of the people, by the people and for the people, in which all state power belongs to the people. However, the government lacks the resources and management experience to reduce poverty and provide welfare services, and has therefore relied on international donors to support its development initiatives. The number of international NGOs entering Vietnam to register, open offices and conduct activities has rapidly increased. In 2022 alone, nearly $224 million in aid was given to the south-east Asian country which has a population of 100 million people.

To legally operate in Vietnam, a domestic NGO must be placed under the purview of a state agency and be subject to its regulations. Permits must be obtained for events that involve foreign elements, such as foreign funding, which does not exclude seminars and conferences online.

In Vietnam, the term "civil society" remains largely unrecognised in the official state discourse. Đặng Hoàng Lan, senior editor at a state media outlet, said she received specific guidance from her editor on how to cover the issue.

"There are notes from the Central Propaganda Department not to use the term 'civil society'," she said.

Nguyễn Phương Linh, a social worker based in Hanoi, said her NGO never received any financial support from the state, yet every single foreign-funded project needed a nod from above.

"Even if we have webinars with a foreign speaker, we need a permit, legally speaking," she said.

Nguyễn Thi Thanh Thảo, who works for an NGO, said plainclothes officers would check every single public-facing event their NGO ran and would ask questions, even if the event's guest speakers worked for the state.

You need to show them that you are a benevolent partner, and that you are operating at their mercy

"They come to check us even if we have already secured the permit," Thảo said.

Organisations are now trying to find the right balance in their language, tone and approach when working with local government. Nguyễn Phương Linh said her non-profit, registered as part of the Vietnam Union of Science and Technology Associations, often invited state officials to attend its events. Right from the inception, her organisation opted for less controversial topics, such as children's rights and disability rights.

In addition, she emphasised that the organisation never failed to credit the state officials first, giving them the floor ahead of others in each panel discussion.

"You need to show them that you are a benevolent partner, and that you are operating at their mercy," she said.

Social worker Nguyễn Thu Hồng said her organisation was no longer interested in inviting foreign speakers to self-funded public events.

"I am so tired of applying for [international] event permits. It takes a lot of time and toil," she said.

While some are giving up on bringing in foreign voices, others are trying to work within the tight set of rules. Nguyễn Duy Cường, a youth leader from Ho Chi Minh City, has made use of every meeting with police to keep himself updated on the state's policy on the non-profit sector.

He said: "Meetings with them give me a sense of what might be allowed and what might not be." ✖

Thiện Việt is a journalist based in Vietnam, and writes under a pseudonym for safety

52(02):53/54|DOI:10.1177/03064220231183819

SPECIAL REPORT

"Even in a seemingly more open-
minded society, many autistic adults
have experienced years of traumatic
discrimination and bullying"

ASHLEY GJØVIK | LIVING IN THE SHADOWS | P.70

CREDITS: Neil Webb / Ikon

Not a slur

We've come a long way in the understanding and representation of neurodiversity, writes **NICK RANSOM**. But there are still battles yet to be won

NEURODIVERSITY STILL FEELS, to many, relatively new and unfamiliar. Being a neurodiversity consultant, I constantly explain the meaning to colleagues, friends and family, but mostly to the British media industry. It's critical the world talks more about neurodiversity and why it's important. Like the people it empowers, the term neurodiversity is a hidden diamond, full of potential but complex and lacking mainstream awareness.

It's a term that was actually devised back in the late '90s. Whilst studying sociology in Sydney, Australian Judy Singer, in genius fashion may I say, adopted the term in her thesis. When it was later published, the word caught on. It very much promotes the "social model of disability" in that society is the one doing the disabling.

Essentially, neurodiversity promotes the positives of variation in human thinking. As a notion it supports those who are autistic, dyslexic, dyspraxic or have ADHD or another form of neurodivergence. The line at which neurodiversity ends is often up for debate but research suggests one in five people are neurodivergent. The word neurodiverse I should say refers to a group of people who think differently. Perhaps unsurprisingly Singer suspects she may be autistic herself.

Personally, Singer's idea very much resonates with me. I was diagnosed as autistic aged 20 and this remarkable revelation has empowered my confidence and mentality. I still face difficulties, mainly in a domestic and relationship setting, but, on the whole, find it a good thing that has accelerated my media ambitions.

I am also pleased that conversations have opened up more broadly in society in line with the term. That said, many people still talk about the conditions themselves rather than the broader context of neurodiversity, and sadly, some still use the conditions as insults. Irish footballer James McClean recently opened up about being autistic in the UK and the comments spoke for themselves. That might be to do with a toxicity in sport, but it also reflects a wider landscape of negative associations.

Of course, role models can create stereotypes and that's why repeat diverse representation is important. Greta Thunberg is up there with being one of the highest-profile autistic people. Her unrivalled passion for fighting climate change has perhaps led some to associate being autistic as having progressive views. Recently co-founder of PayPal Peter Thiel described Thunberg as being part of the "autistic children's crusade" and TV host Julia Hartley-Brewer used the term autistic as an insult against her

Society is the one doing the disabling

I'm wary of freezing neurotypical people out of the autistic conversation

CREDIT: Nick Ransom

in a tweet. It's dispiriting, and ableism is sadly still rife.

Influential figures on the right therefore have the power to harm the credibility of neurodivergent people. I can see why they might think we epitomise 21st century culture wars, but we are just so diverse, like the rest of humanity.

That said, one common theme I find across all forms of neurodiversity is empathy. Contrary to popular belief, autistic people can often feel overwhelming empathy. Occasionally we'll misread a situation and so won't feel empathy until we're clearer, but very often we want to help people, having struggled ourselves. With research suggesting those who are left-leaning

....

ABOVE: Journalist and neurodiversity consultant Nick Ransom on the job for ITV

tend to be more empathetic, I wouldn't be surprised if neurodivergent people are more progressive and liberal.

Moving towards better representation

I love the attention to detail that comes with being autistic. There are details in everything, but these details can result in anguish or ecstasy, depending on whether it's satisfying or distressing. This obsession for accurate representation reminds me of my work as a producer on the BBC documentary series Inside Our Autistic

Minds, presented by autistic naturalist Chris Packham. It was a complicated programme to make but at the heart of it were autistic people making films about their experiences and owning their narrative. Its aims were to educate (the masses) and empower (autistic minds). Prior to this series, autistic people rarely spoke in the media and were often spoken for. On the release of this series, positive representation arrived.

Neurotypical people (so those who aren't neurodivergent) featured too, in the form of parents and the odd expert. A lot of the autistic community feel programmes like this should be made by an all-autistic production team and I can see why. It's critical that autistic people are allowed to represent themselves. However, I'm very wary of freezing neurotypical people out of the autistic conversation. If respectful, the non-neurodivergent insight on our behaviours can be just as valid and important to consider.

While programmes such as Inside Our Austistic Minds are opening up conversations, I am still pleading with the media to offer a more nuanced portrayal. The other day I read a story of a dyslexic celebrity and it was infuriating because there was clearly no balance given to their strengths. Of course it's up to us in the media to find a story and a struggle and all the rest of it, but just please do our strengths justice. At the same time. it's easy to go in the other direction too and paint neurodivergent people as savants or geniuses. The →

ABOVE: Nick Ransom (right) with Chris Packham for the BBC show Inside Our Autistic Minds

I worry about online division surrounding neurodiversity

→ people in the middle are very often left out and that's the challenge with black and white media thinking. It's important to represent everyone. You are still valid if you can't work or if you are drowning in domestic difficulty. We need to show the turquoise, the beige, the mahogany…

Helpful language, harmful pushback

Most autistic people prefer identity-first language, which is saying an "autistic person" rather than a "person with autism". While I advocate for the media to follow the majority view, everyone should have a choice. For instance, a dyspraxic person may find themselves so clumsy while doing chores that they consider it a life-limiting disability. Saying they "have dyspraxia" as opposed to saying they "are dyspraxic" may be more empowering to them. They should not be jumped on for using this language.

I do worry, in fact, about the online division surrounding neurodiversity. Those who self-diagnose are often eye-rolled at and parents who look for support sometimes get in trouble for saying the wrong thing. My Twitter mentions prove the strength of feeling around this. I get accused of "encouraging division" for simply

asking two questions reflecting both sides. Another asked why I "assumed" communities were at each other. In my DMs, a non-autistic mum says she got picked up on language when seeking support for her son. That's not right. Her example is part of a wider one, namely the rhetoric around and treatment of "Autism Moms". This is a condescending name that has now come to essentially mean "irritating know-it-all mums of autistic children". They're the parents who see themselves as the victim, who seek sympathy yet attempt to own the narrative of autistic children. I'm sure "Autism Moms" do sometimes mess up, but that does not justify the vitriol they receive. This vitriol can have a silencing effect. It is important we work together, with kindness, to move forward. It's also important that those who can't advocate for themselves are advocated for.

On the flipside, "Autism Moms" stems from the mindset of the phrase "nothing about us without us". Autistic people want autistic children to be seen as what they are - children, with potential - and to have their own voice and agency. Perhaps it's unsurprising that neurodivergent people are so passionate when we've been marginalised for so long. We just want to be heard, not spoken for or exploited for "likes".

Fortunately for all the challenges on social media – the people shouting down "Autism Moms" and others who are speaking about neurodiversity – social media has for the most part provided that colour to neurodivergent representation. Take #actuallyautistic as an example. It's a movement that in many ways has attempted to reclaim the autistic narrative. The hashtags #autism and #autistic were getting a bit busy so it's become a clearer way of differentiating online that you are actually autistic. There will always be concern about discussing such delicate matters in such a public space but surely the fact people are proud to talk about the subject is a good thing?

TikTok and Twitter have become go-tos for those who want content on ADHD or any form of neurodivergence. Is that a bad thing? Maybe if you're looking for facts, not experiences. On social media, we have to be careful. There is frustration, there is difficulty, and so attempts or solutions to make life easier must be well considered. That is what is critical; respect but reality.

I'm of the belief we should all embrace the neurodiversity movement – in its many shades – to inspire generational and societal change. Talking about individualised conditions will still be helpful in instances, of course, but here's a word, that, whilst promoting the social model of disability, perfectly permeates positivity and potential. Use and understand it: neurodiversity. ✖

Nick Ransom is a journalist and neurodiversity consultant from the UK

52(02):56/58|DOI:10.1177/03064220231183820

CREDIT: Nick Ransom

100 hard-hitting poems about the war in Ukraine

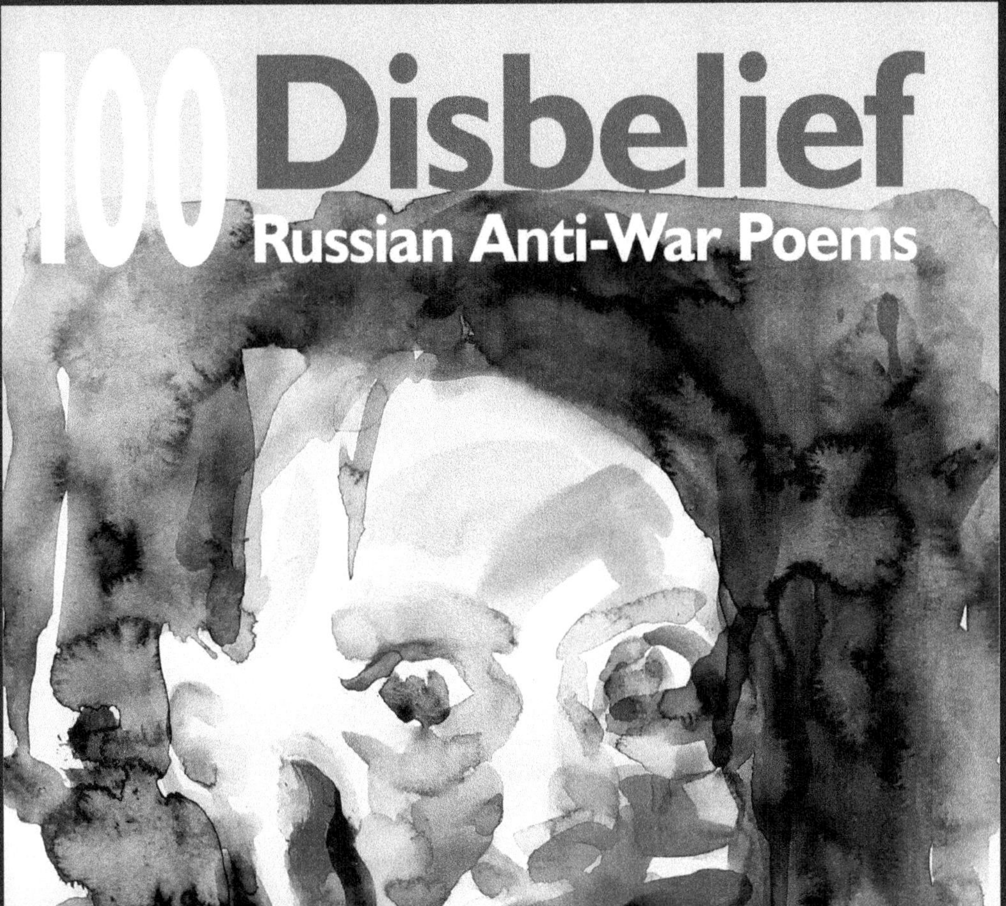

100 Disbelief

Russian Anti-War Poems

edited by Julia **Nemirovskaya**

Including poems by:

Polina Barskova

Vladimir Druk

Tatiana Voltskaya

Mikhail Aizenberg

Tatiana Shcherbina

ISBN:
9781739772277

Price:
£9.99

Smokestack Books
www.smokestack-books.co.uk

Sit down, shut up

A popular treatment in many countries in the world threatens the communication rights of autistic non-speakers, argues **KATHARINE P BEALS**

A PRACTITIONER SITS WITH a child at a table in the corner of a room. She prompts him continually. The child tries to escape but he's totally boxed in – by the practitioner, the table and the two walls. When he stands up, he's pulled back down. When he wails and pounds, he's prompted to get back on task. When he protests ("All done!") his words are ignored. The session is not done until the practitioner decides it's done.

If you're tuned into the world of neurodiversity, you might think you know exactly what this is. The constant prompting, the forced compliance, the dismissing of off-task behaviours – this, surely, is Applied Behavioural Analysis, the standard intervention for autism. Indeed, it's all that is wrong with ABA. It's why, for many neurodiversity proponents, ABA is the bête noire of autism interventions.

ABA was originally designed for mitigating behaviours like tantrums and eating irregularitites as well as teaching basic skills like vocabulary, while in its later application to autism, studies show it boosts communication skills and adaptive functioning. But it has been criticised on several counts: for falling far short of early claims of "curing" autism and for attempting to inflict such a cure; for its intensity – 20 to 40 hours per week; for its drills and reinforcements, which some compare to dog training; and finally, despite its shift from more coercive table-top settings towards more natural, play-oriented settings, for causing PTSD.

But the boxed-in child never gets to tell the world about the far more traumatic intervention they're being put through. That's because this intervention

doesn't teach communication. Rather, it simultaneously suppresses communication and hijacks it.

The intervention is facilitated communication (FC). Its basic elements are a facilitator who holds the wrist or forearm of a non-speaker while the non-speaker points to letters on a keyboard. That's the version of FC that became popular in the late 1980s around the world but particularly in English-speaking countries, and especially with autistic non-speakers.

By the late 1990s, dozens of studies showed that it was the facilitator who controlled the messages. When the facilitator was shown a picture of a flower while the non-speaker was simultaneously (unbeknown to the facilitator) shown a key, what was typed out was not "k-e-y", but "f-l-o-w-e-r".

In test after test, the correct answer was typed only when the facilitator knew the answer. The facilitator, it turned out, was unwittingly cueing the letter selections through non-conscious muscle movements that arise through a psychological effect known as the ideomotor phenomenon. When some of these early facilitators discovered what was happening, they were shocked and abandoned the process.

But FC stuck around. Desperate parents continued to resort to it, those who spoke out against it were (and are) accused of ableist skepticism and it assumed subtle new forms. Over time, those subjected to it become (subconsciously) sensitised to increasingly subtle (non-conscious) facilitator-generated muscle movements. Wrist holds evolved into pressure on shoulders or thighs; and unintentional auditory or visual cues (vocalisations,

gestures) replaced tactile cues.

To naive eyes, it sometimes looks as though all the facilitator is doing is sitting next to a person and watching them type. Yet dozens of studies from the 1990s consistently found that if the facilitator leaves the room or doesn't know the answers, that person is unable to produce appropriate, spontaneous responses – especially ones containing the well-formed sentences and perfectly-spelled vocabulary that he or she produces when the facilitator is present and knows what the response should be.

Complicating matters, novel forms of FC have appeared, marketed as something completely different. By 2003, we had Rapid Prompting Method (RPM) and by 2015, Spelling

CREDIT: Sebastian Gollnow/dpa/Alamy Live News

LEFT: A therapist works with an autistic child on recognition and writing of letters on a keyboard in Korb, Germany, 2017

take ownership of the letterboards – videos show people attempting to hold boards only to have their facilitator remove it. Instead, the boards are controlled by facilitators, as are the autistic people themselves – their cries of protest ("No more! No more!" or "I'm sad. I want Mama") are often ignored.

Many are able to communicate independently. The problem for facilitators is that their words and gestures often clash with the messages they are being directed to type, as I write about in detail on the site Facilitated Communication. How can someone talk about how S2C allowed her to express her true feelings while simultaneously protesting "No more! No more!"?

Anecdotal reports, including by a pro-S2C parent, suggest some practitioners actively discourage speech. Speech, of course, is a lot harder for facilitators to control than single-finger typing. So speech, particularly speech made in protest, is silenced or ignored, while alternative messages, including messages that negate those protests, are forced out and falsely attributed. The rights violations are appalling.

But with ABA falling short of its early promises, and with no other evidence-based therapy endowing minimally-speaking autistic individuals with the communication capacities that parents crave, FC offers hope.

Meanwhile, the public is fed a steady diet of feelgood, FC-promoting news stories and films that win over yet more converts – obscuring the terrible costs to some of the most vulnerable people. ✖

Katharine P Beals is a US-based academic and author of Students with Autism: How to Improve Language, Literacy, and Academic Success and a regular contributor to FacilitatedCommunication.org

to Communicate (S2C). These methods don't look like FC. Instead of holding the person's hand, the facilitator holds up a letterboard. Instead of unconsciously cueing with muscle pressure, the facilitator unconsciously moves the letterboard, reducing the distance between the targeted letter and the person's extended finger.

In short excerpts, RPM and S2C look a lot less coercive than "classic" FC. And, as promoters will tell you, there is no research showing them to be invalid. But that's partly because no practitioners have agreed to rigorous testing and/or to the publication of the results, as is reflected in the absence of any published studies. Yet half a dozen published, informal tests, including several

described in the pro-RPM memoir Strange Son, have shown facilitators to be the ones controlling the messages.

RPM and S2C facilitators compensate for their lack of immediate control (as compared with the classic facilitator's direct contact with the typing arm) by determining letter selection in other ways. As we see in the 2023 pro-S2C documentary Spellers, they decide when and what has been selected, routinely ignoring or dismissing "incorrect" choices or misreading which letter was typed. They whisk the board away when typing goes awry, and when they bring it back, it's often with the target letter in front of the pointing finger.

Tellingly, not once do we see facilitators letting autistic individuals

52(02):60/61|DOI:10.1177/03064220231183821

Fake it till you break it

The rise of neurodiverse "fakeclaiming" on social media is harming neurodivergent people, writes **MORGAN BARBOUR**

ISSOCIATIVE IDENTITY DISORDER, formerly known as multiple personality disorder, is estimated to affect 0.01 to 1.5% of the population. In the real world, DID is often classified as a severe trauma response and can lead to prolonged health problems such as depression, memory loss and suicidal ideation. On TikTok, however, #dissociativeidentitydisorder has racked up over 1.5 billion views. Content creators are seen smiling into the camera, introducing their "alters" or alternate personalities with the flick of a switch.

Often accused of "fakeclaiming" for attention, these content creators have divided the internet. Subreddits (subforums on the website Reddit), such as r/DIDcringe and r/fakedisordercringe, have sprung up to scrutinise and debunk such accounts. Even within the neurodiverse community, opinions on who is legitimate and who is faking it for attention run wild.

Allegations of fakeclaiming are not isolated to the DID community. In recent years psychiatrists have seen an increase in self-diagnosis in young people, for conditions that run the gamut from autism to ADHD to

Tourette's to PTSD. The 2021 study TikTok Tics: A Pandemic Within a Pandemic concluded that the uptick of social media influencers claiming to have Tourette's Syndrome was an example of "mass sociogenic illness" and advised that clinicians "remain abreast of social media sources as they have now become essential in managing patients in the current environment".

Sometimes referred to as Munchausen's by Internet (coined by Dr Marc Feldman in 2000), the phenomenon of faking illness for internet clout is not new. Feldman says he first became aware of such a user in

CREDIT: Vincenzo Di agati / Alamy Stock Photo

1997, when one of his students spoke to him about a monk documenting his journey with terminal cancer on an online forum. When the alleged monk's illness lasted much longer than Feldman would have anticipated, he engaged in a series of private emails with the user, only to learn that the whole thing had been a hoax.

TikTok user EizaWolfe is no stranger to accusations of fakeclaiming. Speaking to Teen Vogue in 2022, Wolfe said she was professionally diagnosed with DID at age 19 and turned to TikTok to raise awareness, only to be called fake by viewers. She claims that at one point she posted medical documents to prove the legitimacy of her diagnoses, only to redact the post when trolling continued.

In response to this, Reddit user Ryodox posted on r/fakedisordercringe saying, "The thing I disliked most about her reaction was that she acted as though people in this sub are just a

We're incredibly frustrated by how so many people act like mental disorders/ neurodiversities are something cute/quirky

bunch of bullies hating ND/mentally ill kids. The thing is that most of us are ND/mentally ill and we're incredibly frustrated by how so many people act like mental disorders/neurodiversities are something cute/quirky."

It is difficult to prove fakeclaiming, and while some clinicians are sceptical, most agree that the mass internet crusades to prove a creator is a fake can be damaging. Doxxing, or the posting of personal information publicly on the internet, has resulted in rape and death threats for some creators. Catie Osborn, an ADHD mental health advocate with nearly a million TikTok followers, has spoken out about the barrage of rape

and death threats that she receives.

Feldman says that this behaviour is unacceptable, but adds that, "the actual sufferers are the real casualties of deception." TikTok creator Tourettesbian (Becca Braccialle), who documents her journey post-Tourette's diagnosis, describes fakeclaiming as "really damaging" and as fostering a 'boy who cried wolf' environment, cultivating a digital world where reality and imitation become increasingly difficult to differentiate. ✖

Morgan Barbour is a writer and activist

52(02):62/63|DOI:10.1177/03064220231183822

More attention, not less

Little understood until recently, ADHD is now at the forefront of a debate on whether it's real or not, with real-life consequences.
JEMIMAH STEINFELD looks at its history and present

IT WAS NOT until the 20th century that the term ADHD came into being, but there were references to those who likely had ADHD from ancient times. The father of medicine, Hippocrates, described some of his patients as struggling with concentration (and thought fish could help "treat" them), while Sir Alexander Crichton, a Scottish physician, referred to "the disease of attention" in his 1798 book.

Flash forward two centuries and in 1968 the American Psychiatric Association's Diagnostic and Statistical Manual of Mental Disorders lists the disorder under the name "hyperkinetic reaction of childhood." It was thought to cause restlessness and distractibility in children, but believed to go away or lessen by adolescence. Finally, in 1980 the APA coined the term Attention Deficit Disorder, with or without hyperactivity. In a revised edition in 1987, the standard name was changed to ADHD.

Today it's widely used, but both the term and medicines given are the source of dispute. A 2019 paper by Dr Sami Timimi and Eric Taylor in the British Journal of Psychiatry, entitled ADHD is best understood as a cultural construct, opened saying "despite all the research it has been difficult to gain and maintain professional agreement on what ADHD is or what should be done about it". The two doctors went onto debate whether it was real.

In a similar vein, Johann Hari's 2022 book Stolen Focus looked at the role of ADHD in our shortening attention spans. He says ADHD diagnoses have sky-rocketed, with 13% of US adolescents given the diagnosis. But he says even the experts can't agree whether ADHD exists and whether its cause is genetic or environmental. What they do all agree on is that those diagnosed with ADHD have a real problem.

Meanwhile online you'll find ample articles

on the perils of self-diagnosis. None of these are without controversy, as BBC Panorama found out when they aired a programme this May called Private ADHD Clinics Exposed. It explored how long waiting lists on the NHS are driving people to private clinics, some of which are guilty of misdiagnosing ADHD. Many who watched it were furious. Columnist Kelly Given described it as a "disgrace of a documentary" that "was monumentally damaging" and "stigma-perpetuating". She said if anything ADHD is underdiagnosed. Meanwhile presenter Adrian Chiles highlighted that "those with ADHD are vastly over-represented in the prison population", that "suicide rates are appallingly high" and that for these people they'll likely wait "forever" for an NHS diagnosis. Chiles described it as "an unfolding tragedy", which could be made all the worse if people stop believing those who say they have ADHD.

Weaponising difference

When the president of your country makes slurs against neurodivergent people, it's clear change is desperately needed. **SIMONE DIAS MARQUES** reports from Brazil

ABOVE: Neurodivergent people in Brazil are silenced by what many view as ableist language, and it comes from the mouth of the president

TRAGEDY OVERTOOK BRAZIL in early April when a man killed four children in a daycare centre in the southern city of Blumenau. The attack occurred just days after a student killed a teacher in Sao Paulo. In response to these events, the president of Brazil, Luiz Inácio Lula da Silva, stated:

"The WHO (World Health Organisation) has always claimed that there should be around 15% of people with some kind of mental disability in humanity. If this number is true, and you take Brazil with 220 million inhabitants, if you take 15% of that, it means we have almost 30 million people screw loose problems. In one hour, something terrible can happen."

The statement raised fierce criticism from the community of advocates for people with Autism Spectrum Disorder, such as famous TV presenter Marcos Mion, who has an autistic son. For Mion, the Brazilian president's speech is ableist and irresponsible, as it directly links those who are neurodivergent to cases of violence in schools.

"We fight for acceptance, awareness and normalisation of all these conditions, night and day. Those who do not have information may look at their intellectually disabled child and lose hope because if the president says that they have a loose screw, why will they continue fighting? This is not only very derogatory but also encourages others to continue using these terms", he said on a video he posted on YouTube.

President Lula apologised shortly afterward on his Twitter account:

"We should not relate any type of violence to people with disabilities or people who have mental health issues. We will no longer reproduce this stereotype. As the President of a country with a large portion of the population of PWDs [people with disabilities], I'm willing to learn and do what is possible so that everyone feels included and respected."

This case has raised a strong discussion about ableism and how the Brazilian media itself has its share of responsibility in the reproduction of stereotypes, and in so doing spreading misinformation. Writer Robson Fernando de Souza, who is autistic, wrote about this problem in the Observatório da Imprensa.

In his article The Potential Nefarious Consequences of Ableist Journalism for Autistics, he points out how "news insists on calling our condition a disease, as if it were a serious and tragic pathology, and treats us, autistics, as poor victims", with pernicious consequences.

According to Souza, journalistic articles are written from a neurotypical perspective by describing autism in a pathological manner with degrading terms that imply that the neurodiverse population "suffers from an irreversible disease".

"An autistic reader without emotional preparation who comes across such morbid words, especially if they are children or adolescents, may feel inferior, sick and bizarre. They may see themselves as less capable than neurotypicals, as sick, as if they needed a cure," wrote Souza. On the other hand, a neurotypical person who hears or reads such misinformation about autism tends to be cruel to neurodiverse people.

He explains that the pathologising narrative in the press brings negative consequences to the neurodiverse "from

the accumulation of reiterations of their supposed inferiority, such as low self-esteem, inferiority complex, depression, disorders such as generalised anxiety and post-traumatic stress, suicidal or homicidal ideations, psychosomatic illnesses, low immunity, and a considerable decrease in their life expectancy".

In other words, in addition to the potential to provoke negative physical and psychological reactions, content of this type reinforces in both society and the neurodiverse population the belief that it would be best for neurodivergent people to have their autism forcibly suppressed and be converted into neurotypical people.

He cites as an example an article in Época Magazine: "Thanks to cannabis oil, the mystery of autism can be solved".

That is, autism "is a mystery", and the cannabis oil is not a remedy that can improve the autistic person's quality of life or help them thrive in what they are good at, but a kind of hope for a cure to turn them into neurotypicals. It is precisely this type of content in the press that reinforces stereotypes and can even have tragic consequences for autistic people, such as psychological triggers for crises and meltdowns.

Another problem is the fact that Brazilian journalists give voice only to parents of autistic individuals and neurotypical experts without listening to the autistic population itself.

"The Brazilian media does not take into account the voice of the autistic community," said psychologist and neuroscientist Mayra Gaiato in an interview with Index. She also criticised the use of the word "disease" because it implies something contagious or, in some cases, something that can be cured, which is not the case with autism.

Rede Gaúcha Pró-Autismo, a non-profit dedicated to promoting the well-being of individuals with ASD, recognises the need to push boundaries. Speaking to Index, their representative Hugo Ênio Braz emphasised the

The use of the term 'disease' implies something contagious

importance of revising the vocabulary used when referring to neurodivergent individuals. Instead of using terms like "disorder" and "disease" Braz advocates for the adoption of the phrase "Autism Spectrum Conditions", which is already embraced by autism advocates. To him, this linguistic shift aims to contribute to the reduction of prejudice and foster a more inclusive society.

The ongoing discussions regarding the awareness of ableism have already yielded positive outcomes in Brazil. On 5 May, the Constitution and Justice Committee of the Chamber of Deputies approved a bill, which proposes the establishment of National Autism Pride Day to be celebrated on 18 June. The bill will now undergo further analysis by the members of Congress.

"Having a day dedicated to a certain issue helps community mobilisation around the theme and awareness with actions that last for weeks or months, directly involving society", said the proposal's author, Senator Romário (Podemos-RJ), to Agência Brasil.

"I envision a future where the growing autistic activism against ableism and psychophobia in Brazil leads to the eradication of these demeaning expressions from the journalistic landscape once and for all. After all, autistic individuals also consume news, television, radio, and podcasts. We too can be affected or hurt by the content we access," wrote Souza.

Maybe that future isn't so far away. ✖

Simone Dias Marques is a Brazilian journalist, translator and writer

52(02):64/65|DOI:10.1177/03064220231183823

Autism on screen is gonna be okay

For decades autism was avoided on screen. But a new cohort of producers, directors and actors are opening up conversations, and representation. **KATIE DANCEY-DOWNS** speaks to one of them, **LILLIAN CARRIER**

ABOVE: Lillian Carrier attends 1st Annual All Ghouls Gala Fundraiser for Autism Care Today in California, October 2022

DREA, AN AUTISTIC, homoromantic, asexual young woman, was never meant to exist. She was only brought into being when Lillian Carrier auditioned for one of the lead roles, Matilda, on the show Everything's Gonna Be Okay. While the writers didn't feel she was right for that role, she sparked their imaginations.

"The writer, Josh, himself reached out to me and asked if he could create a character around my specific autism to make it as authentic as possible," Carrier told Index. "And that's how you get true, authentic representation. You can't say it's not real, because it's everything that I feel and go through."

The character's personality and the scenarios she faces come from the creative minds of the writers, but the autism is based on Carrier herself. While auditioning for Matilda, she wore a calming sensory item — a donut-shaped chewable necklace, or "chewy" — and the jewellery became a part of Drea's ensemble. She worked with the props and costume team to find things that fit Drea's character, but also suited Carrier's own sensory needs. They brought in the compression shirts she wears, fabrics that were comfortable for her and chewable toppers on all her pens to stop her ruining them. The dog in the show is Carrier's own service dog.

"He couldn't tell when I was having a real panic attack or a fake panic attack. He just did what he was supposed to do," Carrier explained. In one touching scene where Drea declares her love for Matilda, her dog Duke presses his paws against her chest as she lies down.

"The way she experienced the world was so different from the other autistic characters in the show, to show that there are multiple ways that autism presents itself," Carrier said. Drea is proud of who she is, and comfortable being autistic.

Alongside helping to build her own character, Carrier consulted on the show, deciding how best to represent the autistic community, which she admits was a tough task. But having grown up without seeing herself fully represented on screen, this was a chance to change the landscape.

"I think the closest I related to it was often those shows that had aliens trying to be human. They didn't understand the social nuances, they often had their own experiences where sound bothered them or whatnot," she said. She related to Spiderman too, because he had sensory and social difficulties, and while she enjoyed the fact this was channelled into a superpower, she wishes the stories had touched more on his struggles. "Those were the things that I connected to, which was this imaginary fantastical side. So having a character that truly is in this real world, where you can say 'That's me!' is an amazing feeling."

In Everything's Gonna Be Okay, audiences learn from Drea. When she says cruel things that she doesn't necessarily mean, Carrier says viewers are willing to open their hearts to her. "When I said those cruel things as a kid and didn't know they hurt people,

people were mean to me," she said. The show is removing those stigmas.

She feels that the TV and film industry is moving in the right direction in terms of getting autism representation right, but there are still big things to work on.

"I think the thing that specifically our show did right is we had autistic consultants themselves. And we had autistic actors. And we have autistic writers. And bringing those things in brings that realness," she said. "In the past — and still [now] — those artists and consultants are often 'experts.' And as much as they can read about autism in a book and meet people who are autistic, they're never going to understand the true lived experience of what it's like."

When neurotypical actors play autistic characters, Carrier worries that it can feel like a mockery.

"Some of them do it brilliantly. They did their research, they were very respectful," she said, highlighting the Power Rangers movie and Fantastic

Beasts And Where To Find Them as positive examples. She is keen not to discourage representation, so her criticism is delicate. "But yes, it can go very wrong, very easily. I don't want to blame the actors themselves, because they're doing the best they can, but sometimes it comes across very ableist." It can be harmful, she said, when studios get it wrong.

There is another problem with neurotypical actors being cast in autistic roles — the belief that autistic actors aren't capable of playing themselves. Carrier calls this "dehumanising and debilitating".

"We used to have blackface — it's gross and uncomfortable," she said. "[Being neurodivergent] is a lived experience, it's something you can never understand unless you are in our bodies."

Where Power Rangers and Fantastic Beasts triumph, Atypical and The Good Doctor do not. Although Carrier supports the fact that the shows were made, she is disappointed in how they represent autism. In Atypical, she sees the main character's negative experiences being linked with his autism, while his positive experiences are a result of him overcoming it.

"Stories are the most impactful thing there is," Carrier said. She highlights how the film Rain Man was the only representation of autism for years, and even now continues to affect the community.

"At the time, it was ground breaking and amazing. And I still think it's good representation. The problem is when it's the only representation, everyone thinks it's what autism is," she said.

"When you're telling a story, and you include this sort of representation, you have to truly get it right. And you have to really take on that responsibility, which I think scares a lot of people out of writing our stories," she said. Hiring autistic actors, writers, consultants or directors removes that burden.

Carrier also founded the organisation OurTism, which has a mission to listen

I don't want to blame the actor themselves, because they're doing the best they can, but sometimes it comes across very ableist

to, empower and validate autistic adults and teens. Even though she runs a non-profit herself, when working as an autism consultant she said the biggest obstacle is getting hired in the first place.

"People would rather hire that expert rather than the autistic consultant who also happens to be an expert," she said.

There's another concerning trend, which Carrier says people have been unable to talk about. "I have consulted on a few scripts that when they are picked up by studios they asked for the autism to be removed," she said. She doesn't blame the writers, who need to make a living, so she has always agreed to it. But she describes these moves by networks and producers as harmful. Carrier wasn't told the reasons for the censorship, but she believes companies are scared to touch particular subjects. "I think often, that's why there's so many coded characters, because networks won't let them have those characters."

On Twitter, autism consultant Amy Gravino wrote: "One year ago, I was asked to consult on #SharpStick, because the main character was written to be (yet never identified as) autistic. Right before I was set to meet with the lead actress and Lena Dunham, a decision was made to no longer have the character be autistic... because there "wasn't any time" to consult with me about it. I had the opportunity to read the script, and the character was still clearly coded as neurodivergent/autistic."

Even in the production of Everything's Gonna Be Okay, which Carrier sings the praises of, she felt restrictions. "Gay sex scenes. Our autism moment, between Drea and Matilda, we had a little bit more going on in the original script and that was cut down to be more off screen," she

said. "But they had a straight sex scene, and they showed almost everything. But when the two of us were on screen, they barely let us kiss."

Ultimately, she doesn't want people to be scared to represent autism. There was a backlash against musician Sia's film Music, which centred on an autistic character and which Sia was accused of going about in the wrong way and as a result being "ableist". (Interestingly, in May 2023, Sia revealed she has been diagnosed as autistic.) Carrier believes this reaction left people afraid to end up in the same situation.

"For the most part, we weren't attacking the movie, we were attacking certain moments of it. We were so happy it was made. But what then angered the community is the response," she said. She explained that the response to criticism was "aggressive" and "defensive".

"The response was, 'Well, we didn't hire an autistic actor because they're not capable,' rather than, 'Oh, we tried. We'll do it better next time. Thank you so much.' That's all we wanted to hear," she said.

She's still happy that shows like Atypical and The Good Doctor were made, because they paved the way for Everything's Gonna Be Okay. What frustrates her are repeated mistakes.

"If you make mistakes, it's okay," she said. "We are gonna be okay with that. Because you're moving in the right direction. And you're trying and we will give feedback — we're an honest community. We are brutally honest. But it comes with love." ✖

Katie Dancey-Downs is assistant editor at Index

52(02):66/67|DOI:10.1177/03064220231183824

Raising Malaysia's roof

JULIANA HENG talks to **FRANCIS CLARKE** about life as an autistic stand-up comedian, censorship in Kuala Lumpur, and their new Edinburgh Fringe show

IT WAS SHORTLY before speaking to Index that Malaysian comic Juliana Heng found out they had secured a run at the upcoming Edinburgh Fringe Festival for their show, Walking on Spectrum. While hugely excited, they acknowledged the challenges an autistic comedian could face at the busy festival.

"It's my first visit so I'm afraid I'll get overstimulated. I thought I'd have a routine of doing my show then go home; but I have to flyer, do random shows, and watch other shows. It's going to be crazy."

However, it doesn't thwart their ambition: "Whatever happens, I want my show to be big. We Asians don't do small!"

Heng is a comedian on the Kuala Lumpur stand-up scene. They were diagnosed with ASD (Autism Spectrum Disorder) in 2019 at the relatively late age of 28. They were performing on stage by then, and already felt stand-up gave a space, and time, to express themselves freely.

They said: "I have this problem where people talk around me, and I have difficulty knowing when to speak and when to stop speaking. On stage however I'm given a specific time to talk and just make people laugh. It's a direct communication."

During their show, Heng jokes that as an ASD person they can only identify three out of the 15 recognised types

ABOVE: The stand-up comedian Juliana Heng, who was diagnosed as autistic at the age of 28

of laughter, while knowing there were exactly 15 specific types of laughter. They explain a joke by another ASD comedian who said they are an expert on other people's shoes.

"I laughed so much at that because we are not so good with eye contact, and I can relate. We can explain our quirks with the time, space and understanding we might not get in the outside world," Heng explained.

In the world of stand-up there are a number of comedians who identify as ASD. For example, Fern Brady and Hannah Gadsby, both successful comedians, have discussed their ASD as part of their shows. Even mega comedian Jerry Seinfeld once said he had ASD (though he later retracted this claim).

As an autistic comedian, Heng explained why autistic people may be attracted to comedy, apart from the freedom it gives by allowing them to talk openly about the disorder.

They said: "It's a solitary profession. We write alone, go on stage alone

CREDIT: (stand-up) The Joke Factory; (portrait) Gabrielle Boudville and perform to strangers. We are comfortable in that medium. People who are on the spectrum, if something bothers us constantly or we have a fixation, then we can write about it."

And Heng's fixation? "Pokemon Go. I think I've played that game longer than all of my day jobs put together!"

A study from 2020 suggested that stigma of ASD was higher in so-called "collectivist" cultures such as Malaysia, where extended family is considered important and a dependable source of mental health support, as opposed to the first step automatically being a general practitioner visit. Lack of access to healthcare is also cited as an issue.

The sense of stigma struck a chord with Heng. They said: "The understanding of autism in Malaysia is still not really there. It's improving because awareness is increasing and more people are willing to learn. I've had some local media outlets want to speak to me about my autism, and when I explain it more people are starting to understand it."

Heng's "safe space" might be under threat though. During the past year, the topic of stand-up comedy and freedom of speech became a source of heated debate in Malaysia. In July 2022, the Crack House Comedy Club in Kuala Lumpur was closed. While the official line was that it was operating without an entertainment licence, reports suggest it was closed because of a religiously sensitive routine that took place at the club. Also, shortly afterwards, one of the club's co-founders, Rizal Van Geyzel, was arrested and charged for making and sharing social media material that was considered offensive or menacing. He was charged under the country's Communications and Multimedia Act.

Talking about Van Geyzel's arrest, Heng said: "He made a joke about

The understanding of autism in Malaysia is still not really there

his mixed parentage, not even about Malaysia, and because one of his parents is Malay (the country's largest ethnic group), people said it was offensive.

"In Malaysia there is a sedition act where if somebody feels disturbed by what you said, it can be seen as disturbing the national peace. It's quite messed up. It's a matter of knowing where you are and what you can say, so I think that is censorship."

Heng points out that at comedy clubs in Malaysia, people are asked not to take footage of the show in case of repercussions if posted online. While they feel free talking about their ASD, there are other aspects of Juliana's identity they must think about discussing on stage. They are also non-binary and LGBTQ+.

"We can't fully be ourselves. My jokes are mainly about autism, but also some about being queer. The autism side

is the comedy part of me, but the queer side is the more private side. If there is something I feel people aren't sure of, then I just don't talk about it.

"If I talk about my queer side and it's recorded, it could be taken out of context online," they added.

Returning to their Edinburgh Fringe show, Heng gave a preview of what to expect for Walking on Spectrum.

They said: "It's a medley show, so it's a mix of comedy, spoken word, poetry and storytelling. I wanted to explore being an Asian, neurodivergent, LGBTQ+ and non-binary person. If I pitched this as purely a comedy show, people would be throwing bottles at me!

"The beauty of being neurodivergent is the way we perceive things about us. There is no standard roadmap, and we can experiment. In Malaysia, there is no reference to autistic people doing comedy. I'm the first reference." ✖

Francis Clarke is editorial assistant at Index

Juliana Heng's show, Walking on Spectrum, is running at The Strathmore Bar in Leith, Edinburgh from 5-27 August 2023

52(02):68/69|DOI:10.1177/03064220231183826

RIGHT: Juliana Heng performs in Malaysia. They find live comedy to be one of the best forums to talk openly about their neurodiversity

Living in the shadows

Girls have historically been overlooked in autism diagnoses. This has led to many hiding their true selves. **ASHLEY GJØVIK** opens up

I REMEMBER THE "SPECIAL Education" administrators questioning me in primary school. I understood they saw something in me that was different. I instinctually felt the urge to hide that deviation. I refused to be exiled to the classes for disabled children.

That was the earliest I remember "camouflaging" – a term used to describe a range of behaviours used by autistic people attempting to disguise their autism and pretend they are neurotypical. This masking can include forcing eye contact, preparing pre-rehearsed lines for small talk, denying strange hobbies and stopping oneself before fully articulating a thought to satisfaction.

I escaped special-ed and also manoeuvred my way into the gifted programmes. "They'll never find me here!" I thought. Yet my report cards from primary school reflect what one may expect – I struggled with fine motor skills and coordination; social complaints focused around my lack of patience and cooperation, lack of interest in group activity participation, and refusal to ask for help. I also fell into a known category of environmental factors significantly correlated with autism – there were numerous complications during my birth.

Circumstances led to two adult autistic women confronting me with my autism last year. "You know you're autistic, right?" they asked. I paused…and they insisted. "You are." I sat down for the first time to confront that difference in me, the deviation those administrators saw in primary school and these women saw now. I gathered resources on the condition, and after weeks of reading I, too, was sure I was autistic.

I have managed to create a life that is rare for an autistic person. I have established a successful career in senior positions at large corporations. I have travelled the world by myself. I graduated from law school. But I can also find myself in a nervous breakdown if the lights are too bright or if there are loud noises around me. I was never able to learn to drive. I struggle to sustain relationships or to feel part of a community. I become distressed at social events and decline most invitations.

I am a stereotypical woman with autism who was undiagnosed until adulthood, even then not formally. Despite many signals to the condition, I could splendidly fake my way through much of my life.

Autism is a heritable neurodevelopment condition with genetic and biological factors that impacts roughly 1-2% of people. Traditionally, autism was thought to impact men predominantly, and thus the diagnosis was modelled for young boys. It is now understood that women are also affected by autism, though emerging research argues that women may be less severely impacted and more equipped to camouflage. Today, the diagnosis of autism is still dominated by

> I could splendidly fake my way through much of my life

male-focused criteria. Based on current research, up to 75% of women with autism may be undiagnosed.

Most autism screening occurs in childhood, so if girls can mask their way through that time, as I did, no one may be looking for the condition in their adulthood. There is then difficulty with adult diagnoses, as even medical professionals can be dismissive due to women's adept camouflage ability combined with the historically severe stigma around the condition.

The stigma has reduced recently due to expanded education and social training, research on the 'spectrum' of autism, inclusive representation in media, and the neurodiversity movement. However, even in a seemingly more open-minded society, many autistic adults have experienced years of traumatic discrimination and bullying; thus, they may continue camouflaging to conceal their disability.

The double-edged sword of camouflaging is that while obfuscating the condition may increase employment and educational opportunity, it also increases the suffering. It requires substantial cognitive effort, deep self-reflection and emotional discipline. Thus, it can be exhausting and create severe stress.

I considered a formal diagnosis but decided against it. The process can be expensive and time-consuming. Diagnostic criteria still do not formally incorporate camouflaging. There is no treatment for autism. The critical use for formal diagnosis is requesting disability accommodations; however, there is no guarantee of proper accommodations due to the lack of understanding about the condition. Requesting accommodations may also trigger stigma. While autism is more accepted than it used to be – in part due to the progress of characterising autistic people as "neurodivergent" – neurotypical people might discriminate against the neurodivergent on the basis that they can't do some activities that they'd view as "basic functioning".

CREDITS: Neil Webb / Ikon

Indeed, following self-diagnosis, I was excited for the first opportunity where someone questioned why I do not drive, and instead of concocting excuses and creating diversions, I could finally explain: "I can't – I am autistic!" But unlike the panacea I hoped the diagnosis could provide, I was looked at like I was an extraterrestrial. I was ashamed and again wanted to hide my differences and pretend I conformed. I saw that sharing I am "neurodiverse" is quite different from disclosing that my autism includes disabling fine-motor-skill impairments.

The lack of understanding about autism also often leads to discriminatory comments or insensitive questions. When I shared my self-diagnosis with non-autistic friends, many denied it or settled with: "Well, you're clearly high functioning." The response was painful, as I realised their rejection was due to how much effort I invested in camouflage to appear like I was operating as most people do naturally. I realised that if I want to talk about how the syndrome impacts me, I will have to invest time and effort in helping others understand, again making me feel isolated and exhausted.

Today – as a recently self-diagnosed adult woman with autism – I prefer not to talk about my autism due to the challenging conversations that often follow. This agency was a benefit of the diagnosis; I realised how much I had over-extended myself and have started to establish healthier boundaries. However, I worry that my silence is another form of self-censorship and may help to perpetuate the stigma. So, I am here, talking about not wanting to talk about being an autistic woman. ✖

Ashley Gjøvik is a lawyer and whistleblower from the USA

52(02):70/71|DOI:10.1177/03064220231183827

Nigeria's crucible

UGONNA-ORA OWOH reports from Nigeria where the neurodivergent are being treated for possession in a church rather than seeing a professional

W HEN A NIGERIAN feminist, Ugonna, tweeted in April about "the large number of autistic people that were never diagnosed due to lack of mental health awareness", it sparked an intense debate in the country. The tweet went on to receive 100,000 Twitter impressions, and soon a flurry of stories appeared in newspapers and on social media about neurodiversity. It was a rare moment of dialogue in Nigeria. The question is, is this the start of more conversations?

There is minimal documentation in Nigeria on those who are neurodivergent. While part of the reason is limited public awareness and a lack of focus on the issue by both the media and the public health sector, misconceptions and misinformation are also rife, taking the incorrect conflation between mental health and autism as one example.

In terms of mental health though, according to a 2019 poll conducted by the Africa Polling Institute about the poor perception of mental illness in Nigeria, it was revealed that 70% believed mental health problems were "when someone starts running around naked", and 63% believed they were "when someone starts talking to himself or herself".

While this isn't about neurodiversity per se, it highlights the lack of awareness of anyone who doesn't fit into a neurotypical box.

Take the case of epilepsy, which is one of the most known neurological conditions in Nigeria. It is widely believed to be a contagious illness, and some even determine it to be the result of witchcraft. This is the landscape within which conversations around neurodiversity are taking place.

ABOVE: Catholics celebrate Palm Sunday at a church in Lagos. Nigeria is a deeply religious place, with many people seeking help from pastors over doctors

Over the years, social media has become a place for neurodivergent individuals to find a community and safe space to express themselves and share stories of their experiences, free from some of these damaging misconceptions. This, in turn, is improving information on neurodivergence and mental health inclusivity.

Fatimah Zahrah is one of those telling her story. She is autistic and has ADHD but she only got diagnosed in 2021 at the age of 21. Most of her school days were filled with masking her neurodivergent traits. She recalls being constantly exhausted and burnt out in classes. In an interview with Index she said she made sure that her traits didn't define who she was.

"I stretched myself way beyond my limits so I can fit in and survive," she said. But the hardest part was trying to join the labour market, which she described as hell.

"Interaction was so hard for me because I didn't understand social cues so I kept to myself most times at work, which was so lonely. It was hard to operate as a non-neurotypical person because my workplaces didn't care to make accommodations for people like me," she said.

What helped Zahrah the most was having a supportive mother who aided her in navigating the system. "My mum did not know about my autism and ADHD for a long time. It wasn't until after university [that] I told her and she started doing her research. But ever since she has been very supportive. She listens to me and my needs and tries to meet most of them," she said.

Zahrah found comfort in a tolerant family, but others do not. One of the biggest reasons most live in silence is because of the language that is used to put neurodivergent people down. This surfaces through the use of malevolent words or degrading descriptions.

Moses Ibeh grew up hearing curse words such as "*olodo, itimkpataka*", meaning "illiterate and stupid". This came from teachers, classmates and siblings, all because he was dyslexic. He recalls being academically set back and how each term, when he came second to last position in class, his parents would verbally abuse him until he cried.

"I hated primary school so much. It was one of the most difficult times of my life, being the joke of the class, being looked down on by the top pupils because of my grades... I think I resented them, especially the teachers who flogged me," he said.

Because his parents worried about his grades, they made him take extra lessons after school. It was one of these teachers who spotted he might

be dyslexic and told his parents to take him for a medical check-up. The results were positive and his parents withdrew him from his school, paying competent teachers who understood his condition to home-school him.

But there are people who are not as lucky as Ibeh – people who do not get the opportunity to be diagnosed or have parents who can afford home-schooling, people who go to public schools where their teachers and peers say harsh words to them because of their differences.

In 2018, Dyslexia Foundation Nigeria reported that 32 million Nigerians were living with dyslexia. The foundation also reported that 30% of teachers who attended training for working with children with dyslexia said they had never heard of dyslexia, and 65% couldn't recognise the condition when met with a pupil or student who had it.

Religion is also responsible for fuelling silence around neurological differences. Nigeria is a deeply religious country. According to a 2021 Statista report, 90% of the population are believers, with Christians making up 35% of them and Muslims 53%.

For many people, the church or mosque is the first place they go when they want help in understanding something. Sadly, when it comes to neurodiversity many receive more hurt than help. It was like this for Ebere (who wishes to stay anonymous). Growing up with ADHD, she was called "clumsy, talkative and useless".

"I was the black sheep amongst five kids," she told Index. At school she would get in trouble and when her parents were told of this they would "whoop" her. When Ebere turned 12, her mother took her to the spiritual director of her ministry.

"He said I was possessed, and if my parents wanted to give me peace they would have to bring me in for deliverance. My mum brought me to the ministry a week later and I was put through a misery I would never wish for my enemy. They poured water on

Growing up with ADHD, she was called 'clumsy, talkative and useless'

me and whooped me till I collapsed," she recalled. The emotional pain of the experience returned when she was diagnosed with ADHD at 22. "I felt hurt. I remember coming back to my house and breaking down, because going through all that so young killed my confidence. I blamed my parents for everything, but now that I have grown I'd forgive them for misunderstanding my condition," she said.

All of this is happening in an environment of an underfunded healthcare system. The writer LynAnn FireHeart has never had a formal diagnosis of either ADHD or autism due to how unaffordable it is but she is certain she has both conditions.

"The cost of getting a diagnosis in Nigeria is very expensive – and not just that, it's very stressful," she told Index. But in order to get free or subsidised medication, you have to have a diagnosis.

"I have learnt to take things slow and navigate life in a way that suits me. I reduce my interactions with people as much as I can," said FireHeart.

Despite the negatives, social media combined with new charities are raising hopes that change is afoot. Can awareness improve amongst the Nigerian public enough that people know they have to both listen and accommodate? Let's hope so. People's lives depend on it. ✖

Ugonna-Ora Owoh is a Nigeria-based journalist and photographer

52(02):72/73|DOI:10.1177/03064220231183829

CREDIT: Adekunle Ajayi/NurPhoto/Alamy

My autism is not a lie

It was in Wales that dissident playwright **MELTEM ARIKAN** finally learnt she was autistic. She says conversations are desperately needed back in her home country Turkey, with her new column hopefully being a start

MY REFLECTION IN the mirror does not resemble my relatives; it creates singularisation in my mind. The inexplicable petulance, which arises from not getting any meaningful reply to my questions, rapidly turns me inwards, more and more by the day…

It was difficult being different to others and not knowing why. It seriously damaged my self-esteem. During the years that I was growing up and living in Turkey, I felt as though I had fallen into a vortex, one in which I was constantly having the same nightmare. I felt alien to my culture and my species; that I was from a different planet than everyone else.

Around the age of 20, I spent three months in a psychiatric clinic. At the end of those three months, my family was told that because my intelligence was very high, my brain worked differently, and I would never be like others.

Despite endless sessions with many psychiatrists, psychologists and other alternative specialists, no one could get to the bottom of my health problems and my "weirdness". With each passing day, I believed more and more that I didn't belong in this world. That was until the time that I was eventually diagnosed with autism at the age of 52.

The world froze when I received this news; I couldn't control my tears.

Autism?… Autism?… So many years, so many questions, so many quests…

I quickly accepted that I was autistic, but explaining this situation to my family and friends living in Turkey was difficult. There is still not enough autism awareness in Turkey. When you say autistic, people automatically think of the main character in the film Rain Man. And that is a more positive presentation. For the most part, even today, autism is seen in a very negative way. If you are autistic, then you can't achieve anything – many people in Turkey think.

When I came out about my autism, some people said, "It's not a good idea to tell people you are autistic, then people will not respect you anymore."

Fortunately, in the last couple of years, some young high-functioning autistic people have become activists and are openly talking about autism. The problem is nobody wants to listen to them. A lot of these activists are still ostracised and their views dismissed.

Meanwhile Turkey now has some autism organisations, but they are arguing among themselves or with other organisations. With little knowledge and conversations still about autism in Turkey – and indeed with only growing understanding about it elsewhere in the world – they don't

> The problem is nobody wants to listen to them. A lot of these activists are still ostracised and their views dismissed

ABOVE: Arikan might not have ever realised she was autistic if she had remained in Turkey

always engage in conversations.

As with many other issues, Turkey is very confused about autism, and sadly the government is not interested in this significant issue. On the contrary, the government make life harder for autistic people and their families, especially for non-verbal autistic people.

Part of the reason for my late diagnosis was because I was a woman. Women are typically under-diagnosed. Many children, young girls and women grapple with misunderstandings, misdiagnosis and inappropriate drugs to treat a misdiagnosed condition. Women such as myself.

One suggestion is that the diagnostic criteria for autism are biased towards the behaviour of men and boys. In addition, many women with autism are not diagnosed with the condition until they reach middle age because of masking, leaving them wondering: "What is wrong with me?"

I'm lucky because I was diagnosed. I'm lucky I have support groups in Wales, and a therapist who is a specialist in autism; I'm lucky I was able to do courses about autism, including "Understand Autism" at

The University of Kent. It is easier being an autistic person in Wales. I'm lucky I have become a counsellor and help autistic people and their family members. I'm lucky that I've learned a lot about autism. I even now write a column about it in a Turkish newspaper called Davul. I'm writing for those who want to understand autism, and it is a first-of-kind column, and it's gone viral. I don't receive pushback, which is great, not least in Turkey where the media has been muzzled under President Recep Tayyip Erdogan.

But I'm doing all these things because I'm living in Wales. Sadly, if I had remained in Turkey, I would never have been diagnosed with autism. Because in Turkey most psychiatrists or psychologists don't know enough about

ABOVE: A display of Arikan's abstract photography at an exhibit at Wyeside Arts Centre in Wales

I felt as though I had fallen into a vortex, one in which I was constantly having the same nightmare

autism, and most believe you can't be diagnosed with autism at such a late age. They think if you are successful, you can't be autistic. They don't understand how autistic women mask and so don't often listen to autistic women. When you try to explain your experience, they think you are telling a lie.

My diagnosis was liberating. It has shown me the gap between who I should be and the reality of who I am. In addition, as this gap closed, it allowed me to see life from a different perspective. I came out about my autism because there is still not enough autism awareness, even today, even in the UK. I firmly believe that if autistic people share their experiences openly it would not only help other autistic people but it would also help neurotypical people understand the many differences in behaviour and many ways to see the world. ✖

Meltem Arikan is a playwright and novelist. She lives in the UK after her play Mi Minör was considered by Turkish politicians to be subversive and to have provoked the Gezi Park protests.

You can read more about Arikan's experience and work in the article "I wrote a play then lost my home, my husband and my trust", which appeared in the December 2021 issue of Index

52(02):74/75|DOI:10.1177/03064220231183830

Hiding from hostility

Index sent a survey to a selection of neurodiversity charities to get a better sense of the free expression issues that might affect people in English-speaking countries. Below **FRANCIS CLARKE** highlights some of the trends and comments

Of the four charities that responded, all believed the increased use of the term "neurodiversity" had led to more open conversations. Of these, three believed it led to a greater understanding of what the term means. However, three said people still self-censor or don't seek advice because they would face hostility if identified as neurodivergent. Two of these, both Australian charities, pointed to workplace issues. One said: "Many people do not disclose their neurodiversity in the workplace for fear of discrimination."

There was a range of answers in response to the question "What are the most common misconceptions about neurodiversity in your country?" Natasha Solomon from Autism Canada believes a link between diet and neurodiversity is the biggest misconception, while one respondent provided a broader answer that neurodivergent people are wrongly believed to be unable to work or contribute to society and have difficulty with relationships and their emotions. Jenny Karavolos from Australian Autism Alliance said there's a misconception about the level of support needed as neurodivergent people are all individually different. Karavolos further explained: "In Australia, autistic people experience poorer outcomes across all major aspects of life."

Two said autistic voices aren't being heard when it comes to recognition and advocacy, with one saying people "aren't using #actuallyautistic voices in panel discussions and on organisation boards." Another said autistic voices need to be at the table.

Overall, just two out of the four charities said media portrayals of neurodivergent people in their country was generally positive.

☦ HURST

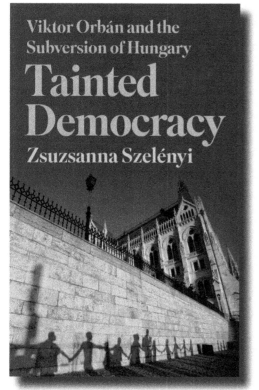

'The right book, written at the right time, by the right person.'
— **Tim Judah**

'Much illuminating detail … Read [this] book—you may learn a lot.' — **Tony Barber,** *Financial Times*

'A masterly new study of the rise of Fidesz and Orbán … a rigorous account.'
— *The Times Literary Supplement*

'For readers seeking a balanced analysis of Hungary's recent political evolution, this is the one.'
— *Foreign Affairs*

Hungary, once the poster-child of liberal democracy, is fast becoming an autocracy under Viktor Orbán. Zsuzsanna Szelényi, a leading member of Orbán's Fidesz in its early years, has witnessed first-hand the party's shift from liberalism to populist nationalism. Offering an insider's account of Fidesz's evolution since its creation, she explains how the party rose to leadership of the country under Orbán and made sweeping legal, political and economic changes to solidify its grip on power—from reining in the public media to slashing the number of parliamentary seats. She answers a key question: why has Orbán been so successful, winning widespread support within Hungary and wielding considerable influence in European politics? And how can Hungary's opposition party Together, which she co-founded in 2014, work to turn the country around? Underpinned by Szelényi's own experiences at the heart of Hungarian politics, *Tainted Democracy* offers accessible, nuanced insights into the global rise of populist autocracy—and how it can be challenged.

9781787388024 £25 hb

Zsuzsanna Szelényi is a Hungarian politician and foreign policy specialist. In the 1990s, she was an activist and MP for Fidesz, then a liberal anti-Communist party. After working at the Council of Europe for fifteen years, she returned to politics in 2012, representing the liberal opposition in Parliament.

To order at 30% discount, use promo code INDEX30
on our website:
www.hurstpublishers.com

CREDIT: SHP / Alamy Stock Photo

COMMENT

"To say that some people have a privileged
perspective, however, is not the same as saying
that they have the best all-round one, and are so
automatically presumed to be the best judges"

JULIAN BAGGINI | LIVED EXPERIENCE, TO A POINT | P.78

Lived experience, to a point

The increased emphasis on first-person experience brings positives, but when it's all that counts we encounter problems too, argues the philosopher **JULIAN BAGGINI**

ON 14 JUNE 2017, a fire broke out in a London tower block that killed 72 people and injured over 70 others. Concluding its statement to the subsequent Grenfell Tower Inquiry, the Metropolitan Police Service wrote, "The touchstone for the success of the joint agency response in the immediate aftermath can fairly be judged by the lived experience of those impacted by the tragedy."

What is striking about this sentence is not that it references the importance of listening to people most affected by the fire. It is that their judgement is taken to be the "touchstone", the measure of a fair judgement. This kind of deference to the authority of lived experience has become widespread. Lived experience is seen not only as an essential source of information, but the source of validity for the conclusions we reach.

For almost any given issue, it often seems that the judgement of someone with more lived experience trumps that of anyone without it, whatever else is true about their level of knowledge or expertise. A white person's views about racism carry less weight than a black person's; a trans person can speak more authoritatively about trans rights than a cisgender one; the welfare of the deaf is best served by following the views of the deaf community, and so on.

"Lived experience" has become so widely valorised that even hard-nosed businesses bend over backwards to show they respect it. It is no longer surprising

ABOVE: Laura Bates talks at Hay Book Festival in 2022. The Everyday Sexism Project, which she founded, places women's own experiences front and centre and has been invaluable

to hear the management consultancy firm McKinsey & Company declare that "Listening and learning about employees' lived experiences is the first step business leaders must take if they want to create fairer workplaces."

It was not always thus. Analysing the largest corpus of English-language texts in the world, Google's N-Gram viewer shows that the phrases "lived experience" is used more than twice as often as it was at the turn of the millennium, 11 times more than in 1980 and 60 times more than in 1960.

Some of the best arguments for paying more attention are rooted in the concept of "epistemic injustice", developed by the philosopher Miranda Fricker. "Epistemic" simply means "relating to

knowledge" and so epistemic injustice concerns the various ways in which the possession, transfer and recognition of knowledge are unfair. One form of this is what Fricker calls testimonial injustice. For example, when women are not treated as equals, their ideas and arguments are not given as much weight as those of equally qualified men and so their testimony counts for less. The same kind of epistemic injustice occurs when the statements of rape victims are not taken seriously.

The increased emphasis on first-person experience can be seen as an attempt to rectify historical testimonial injustices. To that extent, it is to be warmly welcomed. The Everyday Sexism Project, founded in 2012 by Laura Bates, has made the reality of persistent

The judgement of someone with more lived experience trumps that of anyone without it

misogyny undeniable by collecting first-person accounts. Patient advocacy groups give voice to people who were traditionally told to simply do what doctors told them was for the best. Accounts of wars would be incomplete without the perspectives of soldiers, civilians being bombed, refugees seeking sanctuary, women being subjugated, workers being exploited, dissidents being harassed or worse.

Standpoint theory goes further, arguing that lived experience gives an individual a privileged epistemic insight. As the pioneer of standpoint theory, Sandra Harding, argued, the insights of oppressed groups in hierarchical societies "are not available – or at least are not easily available – from the perspective of dominant group activity."

To say that some people have a privileged perspective, however, is not the same as saying that they have the best all-round one, and are so automatically presumed to be the best judges. For example, a practising Catholic has a perspective on her faith that an outside observer can never have. But that does not mean she is right about the truth of Catholicism. Indeed, it could not mean this because if we granted her that authority, we would have to extend the same respect to the views of practising Muslims, Jains, Buddhists and so on. Since they all believe different things, obviously no more than one can be right.

The judgements of people with lived experiences often clashes. Of course we should listen to the lived experience of trans women, but also to the lived experience of cis women. If they reach different conclusions about the importance of single-sex spaces, for example, lived experience cannot adjudicate.

Indeed, grievance is often stoked by the perception, correct or not, that some people's lived experiences are given more weight than others. Such asymmetries are inevitable if people believe in deferring to lived experience, because unless you pick and choose who to listen to, you

People are not necessarily more morally upright in virtue of being marginalised

can never get to a solution simply by accepting the testimony of everyone.

The problem of a plurality of perspectives goes deeper than this, however. Even within marginalised or disadvantaged groups, not everyone has the same point of view. For example, there were disagreements between Justice4Grenfell and Grenfell United, two groups formed in the aftermath of the Grenfell fire, as well as with the Grenfell Action Group, which already existed to advocate for tenants' rights. Similarly, some trans people believe that trans women are women and trans men are men, period, while there are plenty of others who believe that being a trans person of one gender means that you are not biologically the corresponding sex. People with the same kind of lived experience routinely disagree with each other.

Perhaps the greatest test of people's faith in the authority of lived experience is what Bertrand Russell called a naive belief in "the superior virtue of the oppressed". People are not necessarily more morally upright in virtue of being marginalised. In Palestine, for example, there are Israelis who learned the wrong lessons from the persecution of Jews and are now persecuting others. Likewise, the resentment caused by decades of suffering have led some Palestinians to adopt antisemitic views and unjustifiable violent methods.

Academic Standpoint Theory is not so crude as to confuse privileged access with unquestionable authority. But in practice, the former easily slides to the latter. If we acknowledge that a person has privileged access, it is easy to think that respecting it requires in some way deferring to what they have to say. It doesn't take much reflection to see that this doesn't follow and to believe it does is gravely mistaken. Lived experience

provides perspectives and information which it would be irrational and unjust to ignore. But it cannot be taken as a source of absolute authority.

Lived experience does not compete with the knowledge of impartial, detached experts. Rather it is something that should work with it. Take the example of Traditional Ecological Knowledge (TEK). This has been defined as "the knowledge and practice of indigenous people passed down from one generation to the next that draws upon cultural memories and sensitivity to change." It is often unhelpfully contrasted with "western science", which is doubly misleading as the kind of science referred to is not western but "modern".

TEK has too often been ignored by arrogant scientists who believe that it captures no more than folklore and superstition. Now, however, many accept that TEK provides many communities with the knowledge to manage sustainable food systems. For example, the Indonesian practice of *sasi laut* is effectively a system of managing fishing with "no catch zones" *avant la lettre*. But that does not mean that *sasi laut* competes with science. The very reason we know it works is that scientific studies show it does. Science can learn from *sasi laut* but the Indonesian fishermen who practice it also have things to learn from science. To believe that TEK is infallible is as irrational as believing it is nothing but nonsense.

It is vitally important to give lived experience respect and to take its testimony seriously. But the judge of whether it has led people to the right conclusions is much more objective. It should not simply be blindly believed. ✖

Julian Baggini is a writer and a philosopher

52(02):78/79|DOI:10.1177/03064220231183831

France: On the road to illiberalism?

When a woman is arrested for making an online slur against Macron it's time to sit up. **JEAN-PAUL MARTHOZ** writes on what we can make of the current authoritarian shift

"I WANT TO RESTATE clearly that France defends the right of cartoonists to freedom of expression." The French delegate at a high-level human rights meeting on 14 March in Vienna was on message. "We will not give up cartoons," President Emmanuel Macron had firmly proclaimed in October 2020 at a ceremony honouring the memory of Samuel Paty, a teacher who had been beheaded for showing Prophet Mohammed cartoons in a course on free speech.

Does this vocal and global defence of the "right to blasphemy" mean that France is a champion of free expression? According to a survey released on 5 May in the centre-right daily L'Opinion, 54% of French people (and 69% of the far right) think that "freedom of expression in general is no longer guaranteed" in Voltaire's country. This malaise is partly driven by highly polarised controversies on *laïcité* (secularism), 'wokeism', migration and French identity. The ardent arguments around the conviction for hate speech of journalist and far-right presidential candidate Eric Zemmour, as well as a number of cases of cancel culture at French universities against "politically incorrect" intellectuals, undergird these perceptions.

These perceptions are also related to the response to those protesting the government's controversial pensions reform plan. In March, a woman from Northern France was charged with insulting Macron after describing him as "filth" in a Facebook post. In April three people in Alsace were notified that they would face trial for allegedly shouting abuse at the president. In a number of departments, overzealous prefects have also tried to ban so-called *casserolades* (saucepan concerts), a staple of anti-Macron protests.

"The defence of liberties has become the most urgent issue of the time," warned Patrick Baudouin, the president of the League of Human Rights on 3 May. The venerable LDH, which was founded in 1898 during the emblematic Dreyfus Affair, has itself been underhandedly threatened with losing its state funding.

And what about press freedom, the canary in the mine? The press has had a hard time covering clashes between demonstrators and the police. According to the main journalists' union Syndicat National des Journalistes, "reporters have been targeted by the security forces and prevented from doing their work". And journalists highlight a number of other issues. "One major concern is the growing concentration of media

ABOVE: Demonstrators gather beside police in Paris in April 2023. The protesters carry pots and pans – a staple of French protests – which several districts are now trying to make illegal

ownership in the hands of a few press barons with big stakes in economic sectors outside of the media," Reporters Without Borders' general secretary Christophe Deloire told Index. Press freedom groups also complain about the political instrumentalisation of public prosecution by the government and the repetitive recourse to SLAPPs (strategic lawsuits against public participation) against investigative journalists.

"Since our launch in 2008, we have

> **54% of French people think freedom of expression in general is no longer guaranteed in Voltaire's country**

the prefects' protest bans and the administrative services of the interior ministry have themselves admitted in an internal memo that such bans, "outside of the justification of a terrorist risk, are a misuse of procedure".

However, despite these checks and balances, "seen from abroad, Macron epitomises the authoritarian drift of power in the country of Enlightenment," warned Thomas Legrand in the centre-left Libération. In fact, the recurrent images of unbridled violence at protests reinforce the perception that France is on a wrong track, with Black Bloc's (Antifa) vandalism and a riot police that, in the words of sociologists Olivier Fillieule and Fabien Jobard "follow an authoritarian model (of law enforcement) at loggerheads with France's European neighbours".Liberals inside and outside of the government also fear that interior minister Gérald Darmanin's rugged "law and order" rhetoric and at times casual interpretation of the law bring Macron's government dangerously close to the Rassemblement National (Marine Le Pen's National Rally) mantras on freedoms.

France appears drawn into a form of "authoritarianism of atmosphere" which feeds the polarisation of the democratic debate and reinforces political groups and their leaders, from LFI's Jean-Luc Mélenchon to Rassemblement national's Marine Le Pen, with little patience for freedom of expression. France seems to evolve in a "moral atmosphere", to quote Austrian writer Stefan Zweig's remarks about Europe in the 1930s, where the public space shrivels under the blows of mutual intolerance. It's where the title of a famous essay by US journalist Nat Hentoff ominously resonates: "Free Speech for Me, But Not for Thee." ✖

Jean-Paul Marthoz is a journalist and the editorial coordinator of the Council of Europe's Safety of Journalists Platform

52(02):80/81|DOI:10.1177/03064220231183832

had more than 250 lawsuits!" Edwy Plenel, the president of the left-liberal online investigative news site Mediapart, told Index. "State secrecy is another critical issue," he added. In December, three journalists of major news outlets (Radio France and Disclose) were summoned by the directorate-general of internal security for their reporting on alleged influence-peddling in the military. In 2019, three other journalists had been called in for a story on the use of French weapons in the Yemen war. Besides, Plenel notes, "the current executive is devoid of a liberal political culture with a president who assumes the right to criticise the press."

Is France's free speech landscape and press freedom doomed? In an interview in the left-liberal weekly L'Obs, political scientist Philippe Corcuff cautioned on 8 May against a "verbal exaggeration in the criticism of the government" and, although admitting "a backsliding of the rule of law", he rejected the qualification of "illiberalism". This is in part because newsrooms and journalists' organisations have pushed back vigorously and, as Edwy Plenel told us, "they have been protected by the strong guarantees provided by the 1881 press law and by independent judges. In 15 years we only lost in five lawsuits, on questions of detail." The courts have also quashed

Monitoring terrorists, gangs – and historians

The UK government is spying on the nation's historians as if they're criminals, says **ANDREW LOWNIE**. He shares his story and calls for historical transparency

HAVE NEVER CONSIDERED myself to be a dangerous radical or an enemy of the state, and my background and activities would not suggest it. I have been a Cambridge history fellow and a member of a smart London club. I even drive a Volvo. Yet I'm being spied on by the British state.

The monitoring by the Cabinet Office and the Foreign Office includes my social media accounts, a flyer for a talk I gave at a private club, details of a lecture at a Cambridge Alumni weekend, and a library talk with an internal heading by the Cabinet Office of "Not just any cook-along this week".

I know this after submitting a series of subject access requests under data protection laws to the two departments. The Cabinet Office eventually admitted that it held so much material on me collected over the past five years – it estimated it would take more than 650 hours to collect the information – that my requests needed to be broken down into six-monthly periods.

> The inference was that this information might be useful to smear me

What it released showed that my activities were brought to the attention of Alex Chisholm, the permanent secretary of the Cabinet Office, and the Cabinet Office "Copra team"; that my speaking engagements, newspaper articles and crowdfunding activities were monitored; and that information on other parts of my life was also collected. This included employment tribunal and defamation cases which I had successfully defended and which had nothing to do with my Freedom of Information requests or activities as an historian. The inference was that this information might be useful to smear me.

My crime? I'm an historian who pushes back against the censoring of our history by the government and highlights its failures to adhere to Public Records Acts and the Freedom of Information Act.

My concerns about historical curation go back to researching a biography of Guy Burgess more than a decade ago, where I found huge gaps in the record. There was nothing on his time in the Information Research Department, a secret unit set up at the beginning of 1948 to counter Russian propaganda which he betrayed months after it was set up.

Likewise, there was nothing on his time in the Foreign Office News Department, in the private office of foreign secretary Ernest Bevin's deputy Hector McNeil or in the British embassy

ABOVE: Andrew Lownie at The Oldie's Literary Lunch, March 2023. The historian has been spied on by the British state for simply researching key political figures in British history

in Washington between 1950 and 1951 – although there were papers for the periods both sides of his time in Washington for diplomats doing the same job.

In historical parlance, this is known as "dry cleaning" the records.

This was only the start of my problems with officialdom. After I discovered a wartime FBI file which claimed Earl Mountbatten was "a homosexual with a perversion for young boys", I requested other listed files held on him, only to be told they had been

This is known as 'dry cleaning' the records

CREDIT: Neil Spence/Alamy

destroyed. When I asked when that destruction had taken place, the US authorities candidly admitted: "After you had asked for them." Clearly this had been at the request of the British government, previously unaware that such damaging material existed.

The Irish police accepted that they had car logs for the visitors to Mountbatten's holiday home in Ireland in August 1977, the month two 16-year-old boys claimed he had abused them, but they would not release them on the grounds that they were part of the investigation into Mountbatten's murder – which took place two years later.

Even though we now have a 20-year

rule for the deposit of historical records, I found that no files on Mountbatten's 1979 murder had been deposited in archives, either in Ireland or the UK. The Irish police claimed it was still "an active investigation" – despite the fact the bomb-maker had been convicted, served a sentence and been released under the Good Friday Agreement in 1998.

Indeed, many of the files relating to Mountbatten's funeral, seen by millions around the world on television, are closed because they reveal sensitive information about the procession route, who sat in which carriage and other similar details.

While I was researching my next

book, which was on the Duke of Windsor's time in the Bahamas during World War II, I discovered that although the Colonial Office Files in the National Archives were thin on him, there were mirror copies of the files in the Bahamas. These were much more extensive and full of revealing detail, such as the duke posting the commissioner of police to Trinidad after a murder which the duke wanted covered up.

Last year, I requested a 1932 police protection file relating to the Duke of Windsor. Dozens of similar files have been available at the National Archives for 20 years. They contain useful titbits on the then Prince of Wales' movements but nothing remotely secret. The police in the UK refused to release the file on the grounds that it would jeopardise the current safety of the Royal Family.

The balance between accountability and transparency on the one hand and protecting national security and the mystique of the Royal Family on the other is difficult to strike. Once records are released, the genie is out of the bottle, but it's hard to argue that records – which in many cases are more than 60 years old – should not be released.

If our history is to be written accurately, and this is especially true of royal history as evidenced in a recent issue of Index, we will have to have all the records made available – not just those a government department believes we should have – and historians should not be penalised for seeking to ensure that happens. ✖

Andrew Lownie is a literary agent and author of The Mountbattens: Their Lives & Loves and Traitor King, amongst others

52(02):82/83|DOI:10.1177/03064220231183835

GLOBAL VIEW

We are all dissidents

Index was founded following a call for help from Russian dissidents. Today we must not turn our back on those who also seek to challenge Moscow, writes **RUTH ANDERSON**

IT'S A PRIVILEGE to work for Index on Censorship, an honour to provide a voice for the persecuted. It's also a huge responsibility to be the temporary custodian of an organisation which was founded at the height of the Cold War as an expression of solidarity with writers and scholars who were trapped under an authoritarian regime.

Samizdat was more than the publication and distribution of the work of political dissidents that was otherwise banned by the state. It was a statement in the defence and promotion of the global need for freedom of expression as a democratic right in a civilised society. From our first edition we sought to publish the work of those whose bravery was inspirational, as they used the only tools at their disposal to stand up to the tyrants in charge of the countries of their birth. They wrote, they painted, they drew. They provided factual testimony of events at home and creative works telling their stories and their hopes and aspirations for the future.

Their stories ensured that those who lived in democratic societies could not ignore their plight. Their work guaranteed that no one in the West had the excuse of ignorance about what was happening behind the Iron Curtain. Their bravery delivered change, at home and abroad. In democratic societies it reminded us

of how lucky we were and the value of what we had to protect. And under the governments of despots it brought the promise of democracy and the hope of freedom under the law. Ultimately for many, the bravery of dissidents helped to deliver exactly that - democracy - as the Iron Curtain fell and one by one many of the Warsaw Pact countries sought to embrace a different type of society rooted in democratic values.

I do not apologise for having a romantic view of the role of dissidents in modern history. Given my position at Index it would be perverse if I didn't revere the memory of former dissidents and celebrate the bravery of the current generation of activists, scholars, artists and journalists who seek to challenge the status quo and their political leaders. Indeed, Index wouldn't be here were it not for those eight brave individuals who stood in Moscow's Red Square in 1968 and rallied against tanks rolling into Prague. It was in the tradition of Russian dissidents that we grew.

But as much as I am daily inspired by the dissidents I meet and stand in awe of those of Index's past, that doesn't mean I don't appreciate how difficult it can sometimes be to see beyond their association with a country that is currently doing great harm to others.

Since Russia's latest illegal invasion of

Ukraine we have seen a backlash against Russian culture and Russian people. I can absolutely empathise with those Ukrainian nationals, whose homes are being bombed as I type, who cannot differentiate between the government of Russia and the Russian people. I can understand the need to use this moment to address historic wrongs and to challenge a narrative that places Russia at the top, as Marina Pesenti argued in Index last summer. I can understand why the Ukrainian Tennis pro, Martha Kostyuk, refused to shake the hand of a Belarussian player at the French Open. I can also appreciate the anger and hurt of the Ukrainian writers who didn't want to share a platform with Russian writers at a recent Pen America conference in New York.

But this underplays the role of dissidents both within the country of their birth and in our global society. In Belarus there are 1,492 political prisoners incarcerated for challenging President Alexander Lukasehnka. In Russia 19,586 people have been arrested for protesting the war. Their voices need to be heard, their experiences known by the world and the families protected wherever they are.

If we underplay this role, we risk ignoring the personal sacrifice that individuals are making by standing up to dictators and tyrants at their peril. The risk that they place themselves and their families in by challenging an evil status

> I can understand why the Ukrainian Tennis pro, Martha Kostyuk, refused to shake the hand of a Belarussian player at the French Open

RIGHT: Czech Foreign Minister Martin Stropnicky (left) bestows the Gratias agit award to Russian dissident Tatiana Bayeva who protested against the Soviet-led occupation of Czechoslovakia in 1968, in Prague, Czech Republic, on June 2018

We risk ignoring the personal sacrifice that individuals are making by standing up to dictators and tyrants at their peril

quo is huge. When they find the strength to speak we have a moral responsibility to listen, to learn and to amplify, so their stories have an impact, so their tales are heard - both at home and abroad. Their bravery demands this from those of us who cherish the fundamental democratic freedoms that we are so lucky to have.

It is in this tradition that Index was founded and it is how we operate today. As Putin's army invaded Ukraine, Index rightly wanted to tell the stories of those people in Ukraine who were standing united against the tyranny of Putin's regime. In the weeks that followed we found the dissidents, the people in Russia and those that were

forced to flee. We wrote about them online and also last summer in the magazine. We revisited these people a year on in this current magazine (see Katie Dancey-Downs' interview with Russian dissidents on page 34). We provided a platform for them to share their work and their experiences. These people did not vote for Putin and they have been finding all kinds of creative ways to resist anything in his name. They can't help where they were born but they have tried to change how their country operates - through publishing anti-war poetry, through protesting on the streets, through campaigns to tackle disinformation. Their bravery

in standing against their government is as inspirational as that shown by the Ukrainian forces, day-in, day-out, seeking to protect their homes and their country. The risks are high; many are in jail and some may never leave.

Political change can only happen within a country when people know that there is an alternative to a status-quo. In no small part that happens when people stand up and tell the truth and demonstrate that life can change and it can be so much better.

Index exists to provide a home for political dissidents who cherish freedom of expression as a democratic right. We have done that for over half a century and we will continue to do so for the next 50 years. That is our solidarity and it is our raison d'etre. ✖

Ruth Anderson is CEO of Index

52(02):84/85|DOI:10.1177/03064220231183836

CREDIT: CTK Photo/Roman Vondrous/Alamy

Unlimited digital access to the most prestigious

political news and commentary magazines in the world.

Ask your library to subscribe
to the Politics Collection
on the Exact Editions platform:

institutions.exacteditions.com/politics-collection

EXACT EDITIONS

www.exacteditions.com
@exacteditions

COPYRIGHT: © Editions Glénat 2023 Taha Siddiqui & Hubert Maury ALL RIGHTS RESERVED

CULTURE

"I think I'm still on their
list. I don't know if you
ever get off a kill list, and
who should I ask?"

TAHA SIDDIQUI | A TRULY GRAPHIC TALE | P.94

Manuscripts don't burn

A new museum in Tbilisi honours purged poets from Georgia's Soviet past.
REBECCA RUTH GOULD visited the museum

SOVIET LITERARY HISTORY is famous for its purges. Compared to the purges of 1921 and 1931, the purge of Georgian poets in 1937 was exceptional, not least due to the stature of the poets who were executed, as well as the absurdity of the accusations made against them. Within the space of a few months, Georgia's most original and talented writers and poets – Paolo Iashvili, Titsian Tabidze, Nikolo Mitsishvili and Mikheil Javakhishvili – were accused of betraying the Soviet Union and killed. These writers believed in the freedom and autonomy of the poet's voice, and would not betray their friends. Under Stalinist rule, this alone was enough to merit execution. Their summary executions and the banning of their works has cast a dark shadow over Georgian literature for decades. A newly-opened museum, in the heart of Old Tbilisi, aims to illuminate these dark passages of Georgia's past.

On 20 March 2023, I returned to Tbilisi, Georgia, a city I have visited many times over the past two decades. A dramatic change had taken place, and not only in the city's physical profile. It was a tense period in Georgian politics, soon after the government agreed to withdraw its controversial Foreign Agents Bill on 9 March, following intense protests throughout Tbilisi. Had it passed, the bill would have required any Georgian organisation which received more than 20% of its funding from a non-Georgian source to register as a so-called "foreign agent". The terminology itself was disturbing and evocative of the Soviet political atmosphere, in which every outsider was treated as a potential spy. As Zviad Kvaratskhelia, the director of leading Georgian literary publisher Intelekti, explained to me, the term "agent" has a particularly ominous resonance in the post-Soviet context. Zviad was relieved that the bill was withdrawn. "It brings us back to the days of Soviet repressions and purges," he explained, "when merely expressing dissent put your life at risk."

Among the many signs of change was the newly remade Writer's House, on the premises of the former Soviet Writer's Union, which now houses a museum on the first floor. On the floor above the museum is the Writer's Residency, with each of its rooms named in honour of famous writers who passed through Georgia during the 19th and 20th centuries, such as Boris Pasternak, Alexander Dumas and John Steinbeck. On the floor below is a series of meeting halls, which lead to a sculpture garden.

The building, on 13 Machabeli Street in the Sololaki neighbourhood of Old Tbilisi, was constructed between 1903-1905 in the Art Nouveau style by the renowned German architect Carl Zaar. It combines European grandeur with touches of Orientalist aesthetics. In 1911, on his deathbed, cognac manufacturer Sarajishvili bequeathed the house to his wife, with the proviso that she would reserve a major portion of it to an exhibition space for Georgian folk arts. Three days after the Bolsheviks seized power, Sarajishvili's mansion was turned into an artist's collective. In 1923, it became the headquarters of the newly formed Georgian Writer's Union.

In addition to serving as a venue for formal and informal literary meetings, such institutions were a source for writers' livelihoods: they furnished them with a regular income in exchange for specific literary outputs: translations of authorised writers, poems praising Stalin and edited collections of poems celebrating the new Soviet era. Many poems from this period are preserved in their original versions on elegant stationary bearing the blue Writer's Union's letterhead, suggesting that they were composed – or at least revised – on this very premises (see opposite).

The mastermind behind the purge of 1937 was the Mingrelian Georgian Lavrentiy Beria (d. 1953), head of the NKVD. As Stalin's henchman, Beria implemented Stalin's most vicious and brutal plans, including the genocidal deportation of the Chechens, the Ingush, the Crimean Tatars and many other punished peoples. Beria took a special interest in persecuting poets, particularly the ones who refused to be incorporated into his network of spies and informants.

The Writer's Union was the epicentre for many of the accusations that infected the air during these years, and the meetings that took place in this building often laid the foundation for a chain of accusations that would end with the writer's execution. Beria personally interrogated and tortured many of his victims. It was this legacy that led Galaktion Tabidze - a cousin of Titsian

Merely expressing dissent put your life at risk

CAELN, museum of Georgian Literature

ABOVE: Writers declared as enemies of the state, such as Georgian symbolist poet Titsian Tabidze (far left), who was shot in 1937 after being charged with anti-Soviet agitation by the NKVD, were scratched out in photos

who survived the purges - in 1953 to call Beria a man who "has shed so much blood / that he has turned into blood" and to denominate him someone so full of evil that he "turned even Eden / into a desert" – words taken from a poem of his which is translated and published below. At the time that the purges were taking place, such words could not be publicly uttered. Ironically, Beria was himself executed in 1953, after which it was permissible to criticise him.

The newly opened Museum of Repressed Writers, on the premises of the former Soviet Writer's Union, powerfully intervenes in a long history of silences. The museum consists of a single extended exhibit, and puts multimedia techniques and materials to good use to give new life to this subject. As the museum's director Natasha

Lomouri explained, the museum has been in planning for many years, and overcome many obstacles to its construction. Its aim is to honour the poets who have been suppressed in Soviet textbooks as well as in world literary histories.

The exhibit is spread across three rooms. You first enter a hallway with blue panels in Georgian and English before being ushered into a dark room covered in portraits and poetry. On one of the most prominent ones, in oversized Georgian font, Galaktion poses his famous questions: "Who did this? Why?

For what?" Other panels are covered with lists of executed poets and their suppressed poems. The exhibit concludes with an art installation of long winding white sheets hung from the ceiling, with the words of the repressed poets emblazoned on them.

Georgian cultural institutions today are passionate in their defence of ➜

Beria personally interrogated and tortured many of his victims

CREDIT: Museum of Georgian Literature

ABOVE: Nino Makashvili, the wife of Titsian Tabidze, during her school years (front row, far right) alongside her classmates and teacher. The identity of the scratched-out girl is unknown

→ freedom of expression. They understand the dangers that a return to censorship – including the threat posed by the Foreign Agents Bill – would pose to Georgian literary expression. The institutions that are leading the way in giving voice to writers and poets who were suppressed during the Soviet period are confronting the complicity of the purge's most brilliant and courageous victims while also

honouring their memory.

Before leaving Tbilisi, I visit the Giorgi Leonidze State Museum of Georgian Literature, the primary repository of Georgian writers' manuscripts since its founding in 1930. I ask the museum's director Lasha Bakradze, himself a prominent cultural critic, why the dossiers of many repressed writers were preserved

and on display in the Museum of Repressed Writers while the dossier of my own favourite poet Titsian Tabdize, which would have documented the interrogations he underwent and any confessions he made under torture, is nowhere to be seen.

"Does it exist anywhere at all?" I ask.

Bakradze explains: "There once was such a file. We know that it existed because, as the Soviet Union was collapsing in 1989 and Georgians

≣ After the building was burned, the dossiers disappeared from the historical record

declared their independence, the new leader Zviad Gamsakhurdia demanded to see the dossiers of all the repressed writers." Perhaps, Bakradze speculates, Zviad Gamsakhurdia was interested in the fate of his father, Konstantine Gamsakhurdia, a bold writer who began his career in the 1920s, at the same time as the executed poets, and yet who magically survived the purges. In addition to being the son of a famous writer who survived the purge, in 1990 Zviad Gamsakhurdia became the first democratically elected president of Georgia. According to Bakradze, soon after assuming power, Zviad asked the officials in his newly-formed government to see the dossiers of all major writers from that period, including the dossier of Titsian Tabidze. He was handed a huge stack of papers, which he stored in his bunker in the building that is now the Georgian parliament. That building was set on fire during the Tbilisi War of 1991-1992 and Gamsakhurdia was banished from Georgia.

After the building was burned, the dossiers disappeared from the historical record, but not necessarily from reality. As Bakradze explained, when Gamsakhurdia's office was searched soon after the fire, no ashes were visible in the place where the manuscripts had been stored. This suggests that someone managed to get the dossiers out in time, or perhaps they were removed long before the fire. From this Bakrazde concluded that the dossiers may still be intact somewhere, perhaps in the possession of someone who prefers to keep them hidden from view, such as Zviad's wife Manana Archvadze-Gamsakhurdia, well-known for her hostile relationship with the current Georgian government. Bakrazde still hopes that the dossiers

....

RIGHT: A photo of Georgian writers taken in 1930 in Simoneti, in the Imereti region of Georgia. The poet Paolo Iashvili, who committed suicide in 1937 at the height of Stalin's Great Purge, is scratched out

The eyes and faces of suppressed poets are either scored out or entirely erased

are preserved somewhere, and will be discovered someday.

Bakradze concluded this story about the missing dossiers by quoting from Mikhail Bulgakov's classic novel The Master and Margarita. In that novel, which was written between 1928 and 1940, but only published long after the author's death in 1967 due to censorship, Bulgakov's main character tries unsuccessfully to burn his own manuscript, following its rejection by potential publishers. Overcome by despair concerning his fate as a censored writer in a repressive system, Bulgakov himself committed this act of incineration: he burned the first draft of his novel, before rewriting it later and giving it a second life. In the novel, the professor's beloved Margarita rescues the manuscript from the fire, and he eventually reconstructs the charred fragments. Even the devil Woland, who is an ambiguous figure throughout the novel, wisely informs the professor that manuscripts don't burn. Bulgakov's effort to infuse his own personal story of

despair and its resolution into his novel offered a kind of catharsis to which many Soviet writers – particularly those who were officially repressed – could relate to.

In this case the devil was right. The Master and Margarita survived, despite several attempts to destroy and later to censor it. The lesson of Bulgakov's novel – and of Bakradze's account of the missing dossiers – is torn from the darkest pages of Soviet existence. In Georgia today, the writers who were repressed during the 1937 Purge live on in the memories that later came to light long after their arrest and execution. They also haunt the erased and defaced photographs, many of which were taken at the Writer's Union, in which the eyes and faces of suppressed poets are either scored out or entirely erased. The Museum of Repressed Writers and the Georgian Literature Museum gives these erased poets a second life.

Rebecca Ruth Gould is an award-winning writer, academic and translator →

Passion for the motherland

Galaktion Tabidze

Who could erase from the heart
passion for the motherland?
Georgians are no longer visible—
who killed them?
So much bloodshed—
who spilled the blood?
Every kind of plague—
who hung it from our door?
Who covered the ground with their corpses?
Who stole the graves from them?
Who handed us over to darkness?
Why? For what? Tell me:
who darkened this earth?
Who stained our soil red?
Who turned our heavens black?
Who blocked our galloping steed—
Merani's—path?
Who froze the wide trail
of our horse's clear road?
Who was deported to where?
Darkness, what is your name?
Who sent these people to be lost,
nine mountains away?
A strong man,
whom no one could bend.
Who, what Judas,
was shot by the hand of man?
While the wound heals
with medicinal herbs,
literature and family life
become spy dens.
Who is this, who has shed so much blood
that he has turned into blood?
Who is the one, who turned
even Eden into a desert?
Beria painted the motherland
the colour of blood.
Beria murdered the soul
of Georgia!
– 18 February 1956

გულში ვინ ამოშლიდა;
რომ არა სჩანს ქართველი,
ნეტა ვინ ამოჟლიტა?
სისხლის ღვარი ამდენი
ნეტა ვინ დააყენა,
ჭირი სხვადასხვაგვარი
კარზე ვინ მოაყენა?
არე მათი ცხედრებით
ნეტა ვინ გადაფარა?
ვინ წაართვა სამარე,
ბნელს ვინ გადააბარა?
რატომ, რისთვის, მითხარით,
აქ ვინ რა დაამშავა?
მიწა რამ გააწითლა,
ზეცა რამ გაამშავა?
წინ მიმქროლი მერანი
ამ გზად ვინ შეაყენა
და აქამდე ნათელი
დიდი გზა ვინ გაჰყინა?
ვინ სად გადაასახლეს?
სიბნელევ, რა დაგარქვა?
ცხრა მთას იქით ეს ხალხი
ნეტა ვინ გადაჰკარგა?
კაცი, ვისაც სიმტკიცით
ვერავინ გადახრიდა,
ვინ, რომელი იუდა
კაცის ხელმა დახვრიტა?
წყლული ვით მოუშუდება
საამო მოშუშებით,
მწერლობა, ოჯახები
აივსო ჯაშუშებით.
ვინ არის ის, ამდენი
სისხლი რომ დააქცია.
ვინ არის ის, ედემი
უდაბნოდ რომ აქცია!
ბერიაა, სამშობლო
სისხლისფრად რომ მოხატა,
ბერიაა, ქართველ ერს
სული რომ ამოხადა!
– 1956 წ., 18 თებერვალი ✖

Translated by Rebecca Ruth Gould

52(02):88/92|DOI:10.1177/03064220231183841

Obscenely familiar

A new book based on an old obscenity trial makes
MARC NASH ponder just how much has changed

ABOVE: A new book fictionalising a historic chapter has echoes of today

T'S THE LAST decade of the 19th century and Britain is awash with radical social and humanist ideas, from Karl Marx and socialism through to the creation of the Fabian Society and the imminent creation of the Labour Party. The Suffragette movement is a mere decade away and Sigmund Freud had just started publishing his ideas on psychology and the unconscious. But one criminalised social group doesn't seem to be part of this prospective "New Life" – homosexuals. It is within this context that writer Tom Crewe's debut novel The New Life takes place.

Based on real historical events and people, Henry Ellis and John Addington (in real life Henry Havelock Ellis and John Addington Symonds) are co-writing a book called Sexual Inversion, which is a blend of medico-legal moral arguments for legalising homosexuality. John is a character who inhabits the boundaries of being as open as he can get away with under law, moving his working-class gay lover into the marital home; Henry, if anything, is asexual and has agreed to be a "beard" for his lesbian wife. The unlikely pair are about

to court publishers when the Oscar Wilde trial hits and public attitudes towards homosexuality harden. John is hell-bent on publishing and be damned, Henry is not so gung-ho.

They compromise on the book being published and instead exclusively market it to the medical profession. And as often happened at the time, a distributor of the book is charged with obscenity.

People rallying to the bookseller's cause are there because it's a freedom of speech issue. They seem no less inimical to the idea of what gay men actually get up to as those who would find the material obscene. This is one flaw of the book, the medico-legal-moral thrust of their argument overlays that of the personal and the carnal, what the rights the men are fighting for actually means in daily life. The passion of the wonderfully erotic opening chapter never reappears thereafter. And the most sympathetic character – John's wife Catherine – constantly considers the reputation of her family. Yet her dignified stance actually represents what the fight should be combatting, to create a society where it simply doesn't matter. In real life Symonds asked for his name to be taken off the book, which appeared solely under Havelock Ellis' authorship. A textbook case of self-censorship before societal pressures. He died before the book came out.

The New Life is an important work on a neglected slice of social history, one that has been almost totally eclipsed by the Wilde trial. The Wilde trial was an example of a celebrity case engaging national debate, whereas professional and academic men such as Ellis and Symonds weren't "sexy" or "fabulous" enough to garner that level of attention.

> They seem no less inimical to the idea of what gay men actually get up to as those who would find the material obscene

CREDIT: Simon & Schuster

We could list similar examples today of important cases that never get anywhere near the level of media attention as they should simply because the victims are less attention-grabbing.

It's also typical that the bookseller was the one targeted for prosecution, a precursor to when the owner of a Florida record store, George Freeman, was prosecuted for selling a hip-hop album with supposedly obscene lyrics in it by the Parents Music Resource Center under Tipper Gore's stewardship in 1990. The owner was found guilty, while the band members were acquitted in a later trial. No doubt they could afford better lawyers. While in the UK, Section 27 of the Local Government Act in 1988 seeking to outlaw the so-called promotion of homosexuality by local authorities, proved unenforceable in practise. Plus ça change can work for you as much as against. ✖

Marc Nash is a London-based author

52(02):93/93|DOI:10.1177/03064220231183842

A truly graphic tale

TAHA SIDDIQUI lives in exile in Paris after gunmen tried to abduct him in Pakistan. Here he talks to **ZOFEEN T EBRAHIM** about his new graphic novel and still living in fear

"THE MORE VISIBLE I am, the more I feel protected," said exiled journalist Taha Siddiqui, referring to his autobiography, Dissident Club, released in March in French (and with an extract in English opposite).

The autobiography has brought him into the limelight five years after he fled to Paris from Pakistan, along with his photojournalist wife Sara Farid and their son, Miranshah, who was just four at the time.

He had been getting threats as he had been critical of the army and the state. After armed men tried to kidnap him while he was on his way to the airport in Islamabad, he knew he would not be safe in Pakistan.

Later, when he reached Paris, he was informed by the French authorities that he was on a "kill list" drawn up by Pakistan's military intelligence.

The threats have continued – "My family in Pakistan continues to be harassed" – and he believes he is being watched by the Pakistan embassy in Paris.

"I think I'm still on their list. I don't know if you ever get off a kill list, and who should I ask?" Siddiqui said.

He added: "I have also been given briefings and tips by the police and the intelligence on how to deter assailants." He believes that being in the public eye provides the best shield.

Illustrated by Hubert Maury, Siddiqui's book uses only a few colours, in keeping with its tone and geography.

Siddiqui said: "The colouring expresses the mood of the location and my mindset in some ways. The blue represents seriousness and/or darkness of the situation, red for Pakistan reflects a richer culture, and yellow gives a dry, deserty feel for Saudi Arabia.

"The process of writing, however, has been introspective and helped me understand myself and my life and why I am the way I am."

When he was a child, comic books were banned at home. "Anything deemed Western by my religiously radicalised father was considered un-Islamic," he said.

Almost all his relatives have "unfriended" him on the various social media platforms because he has proclaimed to be areligious and they say he has radical political views. However, he continues to crave validation from his parents.

"I want them to be happy for me and be proud of me where I am today, given what I lived through. It has certainly not been easy," he said.

The book, critical of Islam and the way it is taught, is about Siddiqui's personal journey and the demons he fought on his way as a child, from being a Muslim due to his social conditioning to becoming an atheist as an adult. But he said that "it is relatable to anyone growing up in conditions beyond their control."

For now the book is in French, with an English translation is in progress. It will not be available in Pakistan – his illustrations of the Prophet Mohammed alone would be an issue, and Siddiqui fears it could even be considered blasphemous because of a tattoo it

> He was informed by the French authorities that he was on a "kill list" drawn up by Pakistan's military intelligence

shows on his left arm, stating the first half of a *kalima* (declaration of faith): "There is no God."

In addition, there are illustrations of the day of judgment and God as seen through a child's eye, and the French satirical weekly Charlie Hebdo posters showing the controversial cartoons of the Prophet Mohammad that the magazine republished from a Danish newspaper in 2015.

The book's title is drawn from the bar Siddiqui opened in Paris in 2020, which he started in order to provide his family with some financial stability (he also writes, teaches and does public speaking). The bar is meant to be different – not just somewhere for people to be merry. It brings people in exile together.

"We carry out different activities including political, social and cultural events, performances, film screenings and hold debates," he said.

So far it has attracted more than 100 dissidents – mostly political refugees – from China, Russia, Iran, Afghanistan, Turkey, Egypt and Colombia, among others.

"I feel less alone now that I have made so many friends," Siddiqui said.

"I realise there are so many others in the same predicament as I am ." ✖

Zofeen T Ebrahim is a freelance journalist based in Karachi, Pakistan

ABOVE: Exiled Pakistani journalist Taha Siddiqui in The Dissident Club, which he founded in Paris

52(02):94/97|DOI:10.1177/03064220231183843

COPYRIGHT: © Editions Glénat 2023 Taha Siddiqui & Hubert Maury ALL RIGHTS RESERVED

COPYRIGHT: © Editions Glénat 2023 Taha Siddiqui & Hubert Maury ALL RIGHTS RESERVED

CREDIT: Matt Kenyon/ Ikon

A censored day?

The lives of the censored are well documented in these pages but what about those doing the censoring? What do their lives look like? **KAYA GENÇ**'s new short story imagines exactly that, taking us to Turkey where a head censor breaks the Ramadan fast with his fellow censors

DOES THE CENSOR shout at his wife who irons his shirt for losing his fountain pen? Which has remained in his blue Reiss shirt's breast pocket since his Chief gifted it to him?

Has the censor's boss promised to raise him even higher in the state bureaucracy, provided he uses the fountain pen effectively? Sign censorship orders a few times each day? What was the tone of their conversation while their aides photographed the ceremony? Has the Chief commented on the shows he wanted to be pulled from the air immediately? Anything in that series about a secular girl's marriage to a pious boy? On that daily news and current affairs programme, whose anchor fumes at the Chief each evening? That rascal?

Has the censor ever truly supported his Chief's politics?

Is the censor afraid to be tried in a court of law if his Chief is toppled from the presidency? For which crimes specifically? Has the censor fined stations preparing to run stories on a case involving a government MP? What did the censor feel when he saw pictures of the 18-year-old Ukrainian girl who worked as a nanny for one of Chief's most beloved MPs? Did he believe she shot herself in the head with the MP's weapon? What were the features of the dead nanny most resembling his daughter's? Did the censor throw up after issuing the censorship order?

Is the censor afraid to confess to Allah that he played a vital role in a regime that takes bribes, imprisons the innocent and absolves the guilty?

Will the censor enjoy his *iftar* tonight, breaking his fast with lamb kebab in his favourite restaurant — Kebabland? Is the censor sufficiently well-paid? Is he paid as well as the MP whose nanny died in his house? As well as the driver who performed the post-mortem for the dead Ukrainian girl?

Does Kebabland serve alcohol? Can the censor tolerate his colleague from the Censorship Board if he chooses to drink up? Beer? Rakı? Wine? Several glasses of wine? Is it true that the Chief surrounds himself with alcohol-drinking aides these days who find pious Muslims too weak to do the dirty work of governing?

Does the censor measure the importance of his Chief in terms of the number of censors he requires? Should there not be dozens of other censors chasing and catching and reporting on rebels who dare call the Chief a dictator? Those ungrateful traitors? Are there sometimes such additional staff demands, and does the chief, at these times, feel himself part of a sea of censors? Is he conflicted about his role?

After leaving journalism school, in what sort

> # Is the censor sufficiently well-paid? Is he paid as well as the MP whose nanny died in his house? As well as the driver who performed the post-mortem for the dead Ukrainian girl?

of media companies did the censor work before accepting his present post? Did he dream of becoming a meteorologist? Has he become fond of moving his arms while discussing solid winds and intermittent showers? Has the Chief ever watched those segments preserved on Betamax cassettes? Would he like them? When his Chief watches television with him, is the censor offered tea? Coffee? Do they only watch opposition channels? Does anyone even watch Chief's television networks?

A well-dressed censor, an opposition party member, works with him in the Censorship Board, and he comes to meet him for the *iftar* tonight. Is the censor afraid that he might be replaced in case the opposition triumphs in the elections and reappoints members of the Censorship Board?

In the restaurant, he's not allowed to take his favourite table, located away from the crowds, secluded in the back. Has the opposition censor, who doesn't mind the location of their table, truly been fasting today? Can anyone not serving the Chief and his party be a real Muslim? Isn't secularism a sin?

What did the censor feel when he located his fountain pen in the bottom of his leather suitcase just before leaving home? Did he feel a pang of joy and say to himself, "I deserve gold" as he sometimes did in moments of doubt? Did he thank Allah for his job as the Chief's favourite →

→ censor? Would the censor die for his Chief as he chanted in his rallies: "Say the word, and we die for you, oh Chief"?

Or is it rather the case that the censor kept a secret archive of the Chief's written requests to promote his allies and sack his enemies as a precaution? For years? Did everyone in the bureaucracy keep such archives?

Between the table with the two censors and the door stands a tall waiter who used to be a reporter. What are the chances of the waiter poisoning the censor for ruining his career two years ago? Had the censor reported him as a potential terrorist to the public prosecutor? When was the reporter's "civilian death" finalised?

Does the waiter today earn almost the same amount of money he did back in journalism? Might the censor have done him a favour? How does that feel like, losing your name as a person and working in an industry where your name least matters? Is that the censor's fate as well?

What is the quality of the conversation between the censors this evening? Do they talk about interesting topics during the *iftar* dinner? Why does the censor believe that the opposition party members are always better read than the Chief's followers? Does he feel inferior? The opposition censor talks about Donald Barthelme, a story of his composed entirely in questions, a classic music concert he attended, and his favourite television series. Honestly, both are addicted to the Turkish show about the secular girl's marriage to a pious boy. Has the censor noted the difference in quality between his suit

His colleague looks intensely at the censor's breast. Why does he do that? Is there something warm flowing around his heart?

and his colleague's? Between their shirts?

His colleague looks intensely at the censor's breast. Why does he do that? Is there something warm flowing around his heart? Is that how cardiac arrest feels like? Death? The black ink, reserved for censorship orders, conquers his chest, painting the map of an expansionist autocracy as the opposition censor watches its quickly changing liquid borders in awe.

How does the censor feel when he enters the small room behind Kebabland to discover that his secrets have spilled out for everyone to see? Is this the Chief's doing? Does the black ink stand for the censor's sense of guilt? His crimes? His fear of the all-seeing eye of his boss?

What are the censor's political views? Does he have any? Is it the case that the censor has the contact details of the opposition party's chief of staff? Has he arrived at Kebabland on his advice?

Does the censor despise betrayers? Yet does he tolerate those who need to betray in extraordinary circumstances?

His tie and jacket removed and his blackened blue shirt thrown into the bin, he returns to the dining room in a white t-shirt. Is it the case that he feels at ease now? Seated in his favourite restaurant with a colleague that may soon become an ally? As an appetiser, the censor is served, involuntarily, fish soup. Does he object as his colleague eats without protest? Why is the opposition censor so carefree when tasked with the same job as a political party representative in the Censorship Board? How does his fountain pen not spoil his shirt? Why doesn't he get called a bootlicker in the press? Can that change?

Does the Chief really deserve the censor and scores of others to protect his reputation? What was the role the censor played for him for the past two decades? A lightning rod, as his wife said once? What would the Chief give him in case he won the elections? A seat in the cabinet? One of those electric cars he distributes to his cronies?

Those young women with long blonde hair staring at their table – who are they? Does the censor recognise them as actors in a series he pulled from the air last year? Has the petite one approaching the table lost all her income because of an order he signed with his fountain pen? The girl raises her head in disgust. "Couldn't work for a single show for seventeen months because of you piece of shit," she whispers. "Hope you choke on your soup."

Does the censor feel funny a few minutes later when the shock wears off, and is there an awful taste on his tongue? Does he feel like pulling down his pants and defecating on the parquet floor of Kebabland?

Is the black door of the toilet thick enough to mute the sounds of his bowels? Is the censor in pain when he squats, finally, after a frantic escape from the public eye? His blue-black shirt – is it still there, resting in the bin?

Has the censor been poisoned? By the sacked journalist who waited at their table? The fish soup? Was it the petite actress? A collaboration? A conspiracy!

Does he fill the toilet with processed remnants of his regrets? When the censor visits the Chief tomorrow, will he mention the waiter first, the actress or the opposition censor? Can he mention them at all? Too late for that, no? Can he resign from his post? Ask to be pardoned? "I'll no longer serve you." Is he allowed to say that? Is anyone?

Has he trusted the Chief like a father? Someone who gets you out of trouble and beats bullies? Always takes care of you no matter what? Erases your shortcomings, from mediocre education to insufficient wealth, and makes you boastful of them?

What will he do when the Chief is no longer the country's leader? What about those who continue to serve him to the end?

Inside the dining room, the censor feels a little better. Makes up his mind. Stares at men and women, young and old, who move around their table. In the opposite seat, his colleague is speaking into a telephone. For the censor, the people in the opposite party cannot be truly known; he cannot predict their behaviour. When the waiter arrives with the bill, there is a slight pause between the censors, and the better-dressed one looks him in the eye. Pulls out his credit card.

What has the censor signed up to? In that

Has the censor been poisoned? By the sacked journalist who waited at their table? The fish soup? Was it the petite actress? A collaboration?

moment of transgression, does he think of the MP's driver? How he was present during the post-mortem procedures of the girl shot in the head with the MP's gun? After the post-mortem, the deceased's body was sent to her home country. Laid to rest there. Did the censor think of her and was reminded of his daughter as he made up his mind about crossing the fence?

Are the streets full of carefree pedestrians when they walk out? Nonchalant citizens minding their own business, smoking cigarettes, talking on the phone, window-shopping, miming characters from the television series he had censored just a few weeks ago. Is the censor's blackened-blue shirt transported from the bin in the toilet to the back of a garbage truck? Has the censor wrapped his fountain pen inside its inky fabric? As a goodbye?

Is it the case that, on a particular morning in May, the election day, the bins of Istanbul, the streets of the entire country, are overflowing with empty beer bottles? With issues of once-banned newspapers and magazines? A nation in celebration.

How does the censor feel about his wife's gift for his new position? When he places its cap on the barrel, before returning the pen to its rightful place, does the clicking sound give him joy? ✖

Kaya Genç is an essayist and author based in Istanbul

52(02):98/101|DOI:10.1177/03064220231183844

Poetry's peacebuilding tentacles

As the Kosovo Polip International Literature Festival questions its future,
NATASHA TRIPNEY reflects on more than a decade of peacebuilding

PRISHTINA'S ODA THEATRE is in a former nightclub beneath the city's monumental Yugoslav era Palace of Youth and Sports. In May 2023, a group of poets, writers and translators from Kosovo, Serbia and other nearby countries gathered there to participate in the 13th Polip International Literature Festival. On the final morning an impassioned discussion took place not about the issues of the day, which is par for the course, but about the festival itself: should it continue? And if so, in what form?

The Polip Festival was founded in 2010 by Serbian novelist Saša Ilić, then one of the co-editors of Beton, a supplement of the Serbian paper Danas, and Kosovar playwright Jeton Neziraj. The two men met at the Leipzig Book Fair, at a Balkan night curated by Croatian writer Alida Bremer.

Kosovo was an autonomous province within the former Yugoslavia. After the 1998-99 Kosovo war, it gained independence in 2008, though its statehood is still not recognised by Serbia among other countries, including Greece and Spain. Today Kosovo has a predominantly Albanian population, and the younger generations tend not to speak the language that used to be known as Serbo-Croat, while few Serbs speak Albanian. A dearth of literature in translation meant that these neighbouring countries were unable to engage with each other's writing.

Ilić and Neziraj were determined

ABOVE: Novelist Vladimir Arsenijevic, poet Milos Zivanovic, Polip founder Jeton Neziraj and poet Jazra Khaleed discuss the future of the festival

to change this. Initially envisioned as a poetry festival, Polip — the name has roots in the word octopus and is intended to evoke the thought of the creatures spreading ink — was set up with an explicit peacebuilding mission. They would bring together writers from Kosovo and Serbia, as well as countries with similarly complicated histories. The first event took place in October 2010 and coincided with the publication of two anthologies, From Belgrade with Love and From Pristina with Love, translated into each country's respective languages.

Over the years, guests at the festival

have included renowned Roma poet Kujtim Pacaku, Serbian dramaturg and cultural activist Borka Pavićević and prominent Kosovar philosopher Shkëlzen Maliqi. Silenced artists have also joined Polip, including writer and former director of the National Library of Serbia Sreten Ugričić, who was forced into exile after he was accused on Serbian TV of supporting terrorism, and Shukrije Gashi, who was imprisoned for her activism in the 1980s.

Debate has been central to the festival and, in addition to a programme of readings, every year has featured a series of lively panels centring on a different theme. The success of the festival hinged on creating a space that was open, free and mutually respectful, in which sensitive topics could be debated. At the 2018 festival, Ugričić

You are allowed to say and perform anything you want here

and Kosovar politician Veton Surroi discussed the failure to reach any kind of reconciliation in the 20 years since the agreement that ended the Kosovo war. In 2021, the focus was on language itself and how true change could only be achieved by addressing the terms used to talk about it.

Greek poet Jazra Khaleed, a two-time visitor to the festival, described how Polip "prioritises anti-nationalism, tolerance, cultural diversity and inclusion. It provides a forum where writers who share common ideas and beliefs can discuss these sensitive and complex issues". This is important, he added, as in the Balkans and south-east Europe "nationalism, racism and populism are dominant".

Bremer, who became the third co-director of the festival in 2014, is "convinced that the festival caused a kind of opening among many of its participants — the opening of eyes, the opening of souls".

While Yugoslav communism was looser than in the rest of the Eastern Bloc, it was, said Bremer, still not as permissive as in the West. A festival like Polip would not have been possible in socialist Yugoslavia, because Polip is "very free, you are allowed to say and perform anything you want here".

These are things that can't be measured, they can only be felt, she said. At Polip, "conversations became possible that weren't happening anywhere else, and authors gained insight into each other's work that they would never have otherwise had. They were able to see that they are not so far apart, either in terms of artistic sensibility or in terms of themes."

Writer and translator Svetlana Rakočević echoed this. Her family comes from Kosovo and her grandparents were killed in the war. When she was first invited to participate

in the festival in 2016, she recalls being terrified to go to Pristina for the first time in 20 years, but the organisers did everything they could to make her feel welcome and safe; she described feeling as if she had found a like-minded "tribe of rebels and free souls".

For the best part of a decade the festival took place in the basement of a building in a socialist-era housing estate known as the 'spine' of the city. This slightly ramshackle space added to the atmosphere, creating an underground vibe in keeping with the overall spirit of the festival. However, in 2019, the space was taken over by developers — it is now a dental clinic — and the festival was forced to relocate to the Oda, Kosovo's only independent theatre.

Thirteen years is a long time. Kosovo was in its infancy when the festival started and is now in its adolescence. Ilić's novel The Dog and the Double Bass won Serbia's most prestigious literary prize, the NIN award, and Neziraj's plays have been performed across Europe and in New York. At the same time, in terms of Kosovo-Serbia

relations, frustratingly little has changed. Covid-19 — which did not halt the festival but rather forced it to repurpose itself in digital and hybrid formats — led to the organisers asking themselves some existential questions. What role can the festival still play?

For Neziraj, the main achievement over the past 13 years was the way in which the festival created "a kind of free territory in which we all can discuss freely, read freely, share our literature works freely, without the burden of where we are from, which language we speak and what we think".

This might not be much in the scheme of things, he said, but in the difficult post-war period, "we all needed only a little, to understand that normality for this region is not just an abstract term but something that can be created." This festival, he said, can be thought of as "a prototype of normality in this region". ✖

Natasha Tripney is international editor at The Stage

52(02):102/103|DOI:10.1177/03064220231183845

RIGHT: Ethnic Albanians celebrate Kosovo's independence in Pristina, Kosovo in 2008

LAST WORD

Palestine: I still have hope

BASSEM EID has criticised both sides in the Israel-Palestine conflict and says new thinking is required

" I SEE REFUGEES AS hostages," said Jerusalem-based human rights activist and expert commentator in Arab and Palestinian affairs Bassem Eid, who spent the first 33 years of his life in the United Nations Refugee Works Agency refugee camp of Shuafat.

"In 1948 [after the creation of the state of Israel] when Arab leaders opened their borders they said 'This is going to be short term suffering for a long-term gain. Now it looks much like that is much more long-term suffering and no short-term benefits at all."

He believes that those countries who have been hosting Palestinian refugees for 75 years should now recognise these refugees as their own citizens.

Eid rose to prominence during the first Palestinian uprising when he was a senior field researcher for B'Tselem, the Israeli Information Center for Human Rights in the Occupied Territories.

In 1995, Eid left B'Tselem to found the Palestinian Human Rights Monitoring Group, writing a report on human rights violations by the Palestinian Authority. A month later Eid was arrested at his home in east Jerusalem by Force 17, Yasser Arafat's personal security detail. Eid was only released after 25 hours following an intervention by Warren Christopher and international condemnation.

Eid has since gone on to criticise the human rights policies of both the Israeli and Palestinian armed forces and has become a regular media commentator on Palestinian and Israeli affairs. He is also an outspoken critic of the Boycott, Divestment and Sanctions movement, saying that it is Palestinians who ultimately pay the price. He points to a 2016 BDS-led boycott that forced SodaStream to move out of the West Bank – a "disaster for 1,500 Palestinian workers who lost jobs".

INDEX What are your thoughts on Benjamin Netanyahu's attempts to force through judicial reform to strip the Supreme Court of powers and give politicians greater influence over the selection of judges?

BASSEM EID I believe the whole judicial reform issue is an internal Israeli affair. It's not related to us as Palestinians. I don't think it will even affect the lives of Palestinians any time in the near future.

INDEX Is the commemoration of the 75th anniversary of Nakba by the United Nations, the first time this has happened following a mandate by the General Assembly, an important moment for Palestine?

BASSEM EID I believe the UN will continue celebrating it for the next 50 years but it will never solve the Israel-Palestine conflict. That will require them to start working on the hundreds of UN resolutions related to the Israel-Palestine conflict. I believe we have reached a point where the international community is part of the Israeli-Palestinian conflict rather than a part of the solution.

INDEX After 75 years, are you optimistic about a permanent solution in the Israel-Palestine conflict?

BASSEM EID Over time I have become more and more pessimistic about the situation. After the Oslo Agreement, everybody was very happy and there was an expectation that this conflict was about to be solved. Now, nobody knows what is going to happen after an hour or a week. After each round of battles between Hamas and Israel, nobody knows when the next round is going to take place, nothing is certain. Unfortunately Palestinians have been failed by our own leadership and people don't believe that there is a bright future waiting for them.

INDEX If you were detained and could take one book to jail with you, what would it be?

BASSEM EID Two States for Two Peoples by Professor Wolfgang Bock, Andrew Tucker and Gregory Rose. I met with Professor Bock recently and this is the first time the conflict has been talked about from the judicial rather than the political point of view.

INDEX What news headline would you most like to read?

BASSEM EID I wake up every day around 4am and the first thing I always do is listen to a one-hour radio show where they cover the headlines from all the different Israeli newspapers. I sometimes have a feeling that the Israelis report about the Palestinians more than the Palestinian media. The headline "Peace in Israel and Palestine"? Well I don't want to disappoint. You still need hope. I still have some hope but the problem is that some changes will not come in the near future. ✖

52(02):104/104|DOI:10.1177/03064220231183846

Printed in the USA
CPSIA information can be obtained
at www.ICGtesting.com
JSHW070726250224
57504JS00032B/117